On The Heights

A Novel

Book II

by

Berthold Auerbach

Double 9 BOOKS

On the heights

A Novel

Book II

by Berthold Auerbach

ISBN: 978-93-64284-99-8

Published by

DOUBLE 9 BOOKS

2/13-B, Ansari Road
Daryaganj, New Delhi – 110002
info@double9books.com
www.double9books.com
Tel. 011-40042856

ABOUT THE AUTHOR

Berthold Auerbach (1812-1882) was a notable German-Jewish author and intellectual renowned for his contributions to 19th-century literature, particularly through his village tales, or "Dorfgeschichten." Born Moses Baruch Auerbacher in Nordstetten, a village in the Black Forest region of Germany, he was deeply influenced by his upbringing in a rural Jewish community. Auerbach's works often explore themes of rural life, social justice, and the human condition, marked by a deep empathy for his characters and an insightful portrayal of their struggles and aspirations. His writing is characterized by its realism, vivid descriptions, and a humane perspective that transcends social and cultural boundaries."Schwarzwälder Dorfgeschichten" (Black Forest Village Stories): This collection of stories brought him widespread recognition and remains one of his most celebrated works."On the Heights" (Auf der Höhe): A novel that further solidified his reputation, exploring the intersection of personal ambition and social expectations in a Bavarian setting. "Barfüssele": Another notable novel that reflects his signature style and thematic concerns. Auerbach's work had a significant impact on both German literature and the broader European literary scene. His realistic portrayal of peasant life influenced later writers and contributed to the development of social realism. Despite facing challenges due to his Jewish heritage, Auerbach maintained a prominent position in the literary world, and his works continued to be read and appreciated long after his death. Berthold Auerbach remains an important figure in the canon of 19th-century literature, celebrated for his contributions to the portrayal of rural life and his advocacy for social justice through literature.

CONTENTS

CHAPTER I

Life at the palace again moved in its wonted channel. Bulletins as to the condition of the queen and the crown prince, were no longer issued. The amnesty which had been proclaimed in consequence of the happy event, had been received with satisfaction throughout the land.

Irma spent much of her time in the crown prince's apartments, and endeavored to enter into the feelings of the peasant woman who had been transplanted into a world that was entirely new and strange to her. She was greatly amused by the droll conceits that this new life awakened in Walpurga. Her peculiar way of looking at things was frequently in accord with Walpurga's simple-minded notions, and when Irma was absent, the nurse would speak to the child for hours, endeavoring, as it were, to outdo herself with all sorts of droll expressions which, eccentric as they were, failed to satisfy her.

A strong and deep spring of happiness and content, earnest resolve and all that makes men true, welled up from Walpurga's soul and ministered to the benefit of the babe that she had pressed to her bosom; the child had become as a part of herself.

With constant regularity the prince was daily carried to the queen. That was the event of the day, after which life, in the crown prince's apartments, went on in its usual course.

Doctor Gunther now relaxed his orders; for one day, he said: "The weather is charming, and it will do the prince good to send him out of doors a little while. We will arrange it in this way:--At eleven o'clock, you can drive out with Walpurga and the prince, as far as the Nymph's Grove. Arrived there, you can walk about with the child under the pines, or can sit down, if you wish to do so. After remaining there about half an hour, you will return and at once remove to the new apartments. You have taken good care of yourself, Walpurga; continue to do so. Let nothing move you from your accustomed ways, and you will continue to afford pleasure to all of us, as well as to yourself."

Walpurga was quite beside herself with happiness. "We're going out riding," said she to the child, when the physician had left. "God sends you everything good while you are asleep. But you'll let me have some, too, won't you? for you've a good heart, and I've given you mine."

Walpurga would have continued in this vein for a long while, but Mademoiselle Kramer came up and, while gently patting her cheeks, said: "You'll have red cheeks again. Show your love for the prince, with calmness and moderation, and not with such extravagant expressions."

"You're right," said Walpurga. "It's true; I'm not always so. I was always cheerful, but prudent at the same time: not so giddy as I now am," said she, after she had walked up and down the room several times, and at last sat down by the window. "I'll tell you what ails me."

"Indeed, does anything ail you?"

"Yes, the worst of all ills. I've nothing to do. I don't know what to put my hands to. This constant talking, dressing and undressing, eating and drinking, with nothing else to do, makes me stupid. The next time the doctor comes, tell him to give me some work. I'll carry wood or do anything that is to be done. They're mowing the grass in the palace garden, and if I could only be down there with them, I'd feel the better of it. No man could beat me at mowing grass. Grubersepp often used to say that the women sharpened their scythes seven times as often as the men, but that never happened with me."

"Oh, that would never do. But I shall see that you get some exercise."

"Come, you're to go out of doors, into the fresh air," said Walpurga to the prince.

"Thy cage is open! Fly away,
Far o'er land and sea.
But tell me, birdie; tell me pray,--
Where can my darling be?"

"What a pity that the birds have stopped singing. Yes, dear child, they only sing so long as there are young ones in the nest; but I shall have you in my nest for a whole year, and I'll sing better than the birds could,"--and she sang:

"Ah, blissful is the tender tie
That binds me, love, to thee,
And swiftly speed the hours by
When thou art near to me.

"My heart doth bear a burden, love,
And thou hast placed it there--
And I would wager e'en my life
That none doth heavier bear."

"Brava! charming!" said Countess Irma, entering the room. "I should like to learn that song. Sing it again."

Walpurga repeated it and, at the second verse, Irma joined in the song.

"It doesn't really suit a child," said Walpurga, "but what does such a youngster know about lowing cows or singing birds? It's all one to him. We're going out riding to-day. Do you go with us?"

"I would be glad to ride with you, but I may not," replied Countess Irma.

"Then you're not allowed to do whatever you please."

Her words surprised Irma: "What do you mean?" asked she, sharply.

"Forgive me, if I've said anything stupid. I only meant to say you're in service as well as the rest of us. You're a maid of honor, I believe."

"All must serve some one; the king and queen serve God."

"We must all do that."

"Yes, but princes have a much harder time of it than we, for theirs is a far greater responsibility. But what am I saying? You ought to feel happy that you needn't know everything. I've brought some writing copies for you. I owe you thanks for one thing, already. Ever since I've resolved to teach you, my own writing has become far plainer than before--"

Irma suddenly checked herself, for she realized the full force of what she had been saying, and continued: "for you are to learn it thoroughly."

Baum came to announce that the carriage was waiting. Irma left, saying that she would meet Walpurga in the park.

They now went out and Baum let down the carriage steps for them. Mademoiselle Kramer, who was the first to enter, held the child until Walpurga had seated herself. Baum jumped up behind and took his place beside the second lackey; the four horses stepped out and the carriage started.

"Are we driving?" asked Walpurga.

"Certainly."

"It seems like flying. I can't hear the least rumbling of the wheels."

"Of course you can't. The tires are covered with india-rubber."

"And so they wear cloth shoes just as we do when we walk on smooth floors. Oh, how clever they all are here. Out yonder, they don't know a thing. They live just like cattle; the only difference is they don't eat grass--but what's the matter?" said she, starting with fright. "They're beating the drums and the soldiers are rushing toward us. Is there a fire somewhere?"

"That's on our account. The guard always present arms when a member of the royal family passes by--watch them. They're presenting arms and after we've passed they'll lay their muskets aside and return to the guardroom. Their regiment is known as the crown prince's, for it belongs to him."

"And so he'll have live soldiers to play with when he grows up."

Mademoiselle Kramer showed all the self-command befitting one who could boast of a line of sixteen ancestors. A slight start and an odd, nervous twitching of the features, as if suppressing a yawn, were the only visible effects of Walpurga's words. But of laughter there was not a sign. An upper servant of the right sort must hear and see all that is going on, and yet stand by as if he were no more than the table or plate that can be moved about at will; and although Walpurga was not her superior, it would not do to laugh at her, for she was nurse to his royal highness the crown prince. Mademoiselle Kramer therefore refrained from laughing, and, as if to evade answering, merely said: "When we pass the guard on our way home, the same thing will happen again."

"And may I ask what's the good of it all?"

"Certainly; there is a good reason for everything, and this serves to accustom the people, and especially the soldiers, to show proper respect to their superiors."

"But our prince don't know anything of that."

"We must show our respect for him, even though he know nothing of it; and now let me tell you something which it would be well for you to know. Whenever you speak or think of their majesties, the king and queen, let it be as 'his majesty' or 'her majesty,' but never simply as king and queen, so that you may never so far forget yourself as to speak of them in a disrespectful manner. Bear this in mind."

Walpurga scarcely heard a word of what she said.

"Oh, Lord!" she exclaimed, "how wisely they've arranged everything. It must have taken many thousand years before they could get so far."

"It has, indeed. But you needn't nod to everyone you see bowing. It isn't meant for you."

"But I'd like to do it for my prince, until he can attend to it himself. They all show how glad they'll be to get a look at him. They all bow to you, my child--you're well off, indeed--oh, what a lovely carriage this is. It's as soft as a bed, and as comfortable as a room, and you can sit here and see all that's going on outside, and--dear me, how fast we're going."

They turned into the park. The carriage drove slowly while they passed the lake, and Walpurga was ever saying:

"I feel as if I were in fairyland."

They alighted by the shady and fragrant Grove of the Nymphs. As soon as she had left the carriage, Walpurga, who was carrying the child in her arms, said:

"Open your eyes! Look about you! The whole world's yours. There are trees and meadows and, overhead the blue sky. But your father can't give you that; you'll have to earn it by being good, and if you and I both remain good, we'll meet again, up above."

"Sit down here, Walpurga, and pray cease talking," said Mademoiselle Kramer.

She was terribly anxious about Walpurga, who talked incessantly and incoherently, and was as unmanageable as a young foal that had just been let loose in the meadow.

For this reason, Mademoiselle Kramer again remarked: "Speak softly, and address all your remarks to me. I should be sorry if the lackeys behind us were making sport of you. Do you see the outrider over there? He is my nephew." Walpurga had not, until then, noticed that two lackeys, one of whom was Baum, were following them. The carriage was being driven up and down the side avenues. Suddenly Walpurga stopped, as if spellbound, before a marble figure.

"Isn't it beautiful?" asked Mademoiselle Kramer.

"Fie!" replied Walpurga. "It's abominable; and to think of men and women walking about here and looking at such an object."

When the old king had the statues placed in the park, Mademoiselle Kramer had deemed them objectionable, but as their majesties had found them beautiful, she had gradually come to look upon them in the same light.

They went into a side avenue, where Walpurga sat down on a bench and, falling into a reverie, soon knew as little of the world as did the child in her arms.

"Who's there?" said she, as if awakened from sleep.

Riding between two horsemen, she beheld a lady mounted on a glossy black steed. Her riding-habit was of blue and the long flowing veil fastened to her hat was of the same color.

"It looks like the countess."

"It is she, and now they dismount. His majesty the king and their royal highnesses the hereditary prince and princess, are with her. They are coming this way," said Mademoiselle Kramer. "Keep your seat. As nurse, you need not trouble about being polite."

But Walpurga could not help putting her hands up to her hat, in order to feel whether the tassel at the back and the flowers in front were still in place.

Mademoiselle Kramer begged their highnesses not to look at the sleeping child, lest they might awaken it.

Irma was the first to speak. "How deeply significant are all of nature's laws. The waking eye arouses the sleeping child. In the depths of every human soul, an infant soul rests sleeping, and it is not well to permit either sympathy or idle curiosity to disturb it."

"I would like to know how you always manage to have such original thoughts," replied the king.

"I don't know," replied Irma, playing with her riding-whip. "I've courage enough to say what I think, and that passes for originality. Nearly all human beings are changelings. They were changed while in the cradle of education."

The king laughed. Walpurga, however, quickly turned her thumbs inward, and said:

"Changelings. It's wrong to speak of anything of that sort before a child that's less than seven months old, for the evil spirits are all powerful up to that time, even if the child is christened."

In order to exorcise any evil spell from the child, she breathed upon it thrice.

The princess looked sadly at the nurse and the child, but did not utter a word.

"I don't understand a word of what the nurse says," remarked the hereditary prince.

Walpurga blushed scarlet.

"Why do you look at me so?" asked Countess Irma, "don't you know me?"

"Of course I do, but do you know who you look like? like the Lady of the Lake. When she rises from the waves, her dress hangs about her in a sea of folds just like yours."

Irma laughed, while she, in High German, told the prince and princess what the nurse had been saying. The prince nodded to Walpurga much as he would have done with a dumb animal to which he could not render himself intelligible.

"But Countess Irma's feet are not swan's feet. Don't believe that, Walpurga," said the king laughing. "Come, 'Lady of the Lake.'"

They mounted their horses and rode away.

It was time for the prince to return.

On their return, they at once repaired to the new apartments on the ground floor, into which everything had been removed during their absence.

They now had sunlight at all hours of the day. The apartments opened out on the park, where the blackbird sang in the broad daylight, and where the breezes were laden with the odor of the orange bushes. Tall trees were whispering in the wind and a great fountain was constantly murmuring and plashing.

Walpurga was quite happy, and the fountain was her greatest delight.

"It's far more comfortable on the first floor," she would often say; "I feel as if I'd just returned from a long journey. The rooms are so nice and cool, and my night-watchman sleeps in the daytime just as a night-watchman should, and--and--"

And Walpurga, too, fell asleep, although 'twas daylight.

CHAPTER II

Walpurga soon accustomed herself to her changed mode of life. She was often concerned because she received no tidings from home.

But if there were no letters, there was a messenger at all events. A servant entered the room and said:

"There's a woman outside, who comes from the same place as Walpurga. She wishes to speak to you for a few moments."

"I'll go to her. Who is it?"

"No," said Mademoiselle Kramer; "receive her here."

The servant went out at once, and returned, bringing old Zenza with him.

"Oh, is it you, Zenza? Have you brought me anything from my child, my husband, or my mother? For God's sake, has anything happened? Are they sick?"

"No, they're all well, thank God, and send their love to you."

Walpurga, with an affectionate glance, gazed into Zenza's cunning eyes, which now seemed good and truthful, because they had seen her child. Smiling, Zenza went on to say:

"I'm glad you still know me. How bad the folks are. They told me you wouldn't recognize me, because you'd become a fine lady. But no, you always were a good girl, and I've always said so."

"Yes, yes, that's all very well; but what do you want of me?"

"I want you to help me. If you don't, my son Thomas will take his life and I'll drown myself in the lake. You'll help me, won't you? See, I'm kneeling at your feet. You must help me. Your dear father and I were almost cousins, and if your father were alive, he'd say what he's now calling down to you from heaven--'Walpurga, if you don't help Zenza, I'll never forgive you.'"

"Get up! What's the matter? How can I help you?"

"I won't get up. I'll die at your feet unless you promise to help me."

"I'll do all I can for you."

Mademoiselle Kramer interposed and said that unless Zenza would calm herself, she would not be allowed to remain in the room another moment.

Zenza arose and asked:

"Is that the queen?"

Walpurga and Mademoiselle Kramer laughed at her question, and Zenza at last made known her wish.

Her son Thomas, she said, was standing down there before the palace, as the guard would not allow him to enter. He had been caught poaching and, as it was his second offense, he had been sentenced to two years' imprisonment. And yet he was not to blame. It lay in his blood. He must go hunting. His father had been that way before him. He had only shot one little chamois buck and for that he was to go to jail again. He had sworn an oath that, before he would let them lock him up, he would take his own life or else commit a murder, so that they might behead him at once; and Zenza went on to say that Walpurga would have two,--nay, three human lives on her conscience if she did not help them; that Walpurga must procure her an audience with the king or queen, so that she might, on her knees, beg them for mercy.

"Your husband and the landlord of the Chamois sent me," added Zenza, "and they both say it'll be easy enough for you to help me, and if you do, I'll be your slave as long as I live."

"Yes, I'd like to help you, but I can't see how. Things are not managed here as they are at home."

"Oh, you can find a way, quick enough. You're clever, the whole neighborhood says so; and I've known it ever so long, and said so, too, on last St. Leonard's day. Schenck, the tailor will bear me witness, and so will Spinnerwastl, too; 'Walpurga bears herself,' said I, 'as if she were one of the lowliest, but she's the first in the whole neighborhood. You'll all live to see what becomes of her. Her wisdom and her goodness will show themselves.' Now, Walpurga, you'll help me: won't you."

"Yes, as soon as there's a chance."

"But I can't wait. Thomas is to go to jail to-morrow, at daybreak, and, if he's not released to-day, there will be murder."

"My dear woman," interposed Mademoiselle Kramer, "his majesty the king declared a general amnesty at the birth of the crown prince. That covers your son's case, does it not?"

"No; that's the very trouble. All the courts in the country are against my Thomas. Look at this. It's all there. The innkeeper wrote it down, better than I can tell you. The writing must reach the king before noon, or it'll be too late. My son Thomas is walking up and down out there, and it's an even chance whether he goes to heaven or hell. He's got a double-barreled pistol with him, and he'll shoot the first man he looks at and himself, too, before this very palace, if I go out there without having done anything for him."

"Yes, but I can't run up to the king as I would to the innkeeper, or I'd gladly do it."

"I must sit down, my knees are breaking under me," exclaimed Zenza; and Mademoiselle Kramer hurried to bring her a chair. And while she sat there with drooping head, great tears dropped upon the bony, thick-veined hands that lay folded on her knees.

Walpurga motioned to Mademoiselle Kramer, who was trying to console the old woman. She wanted to tell her that Zenza was not so very good, after all, and that Thomas was still worse; but Mademoiselle Kramer turned about and said:

"I have an idea. Countess Wildenort's brother is aid-de-camp to his majesty, and, in half an hour from now, will present his report and get the countersign. Now, Walpurga, go to Countess Irma at once and request her to hand the petition to her brother, so that he may submit it to his majesty."

"Yes, yes, do go--do! Lord, what a wise angel you have here with you, Walpurga;--but go right off--don't lose a moment! May I stay here a little while longer, or shall I wait down there before the palace?"

"No! you may remain here, my good woman," said Mademoiselle Kramer, consoling her. "But hurry yourself," said she, addressing Walpurga, who still held the letter before her, and stood there as if immovable.

Walpurga left the apartment. When she drew near to Irma's door, she heard the countess, with fervid expression, singing Schumann's song to Friedrich Rueckert's words:

He came to me,
In storm and rain,
And boldly, he

My heart hath ta'en.

Was my heart won,
Or his, that day?
Methinks both hearts
Did meet half-way.

The chambermaid announced Walpurga. Irma stopped in the middle of her song.

"Welcome! What good thought brings you here?"

Walpurga hesitated, but, at last, preferred her request and handed the paper to the countess.

"Take courage," said Irma, consolingly.

She rang for a servant, to whom she said: "Tell my brother to come here at once." Then, addressing Walpurga, she continued: "I'll add a few words of my own. Be calm. I am glad to be able to grant your request. I've often wanted to ask you whether there was not some wish that you would like to have gratified. The king will surely grant the pardon."

Walpurga would have liked to interrupt her, but everything seemed as if bewitched. Before she could say a word, the aid-de-camp had come. Irma begged him to wait while she added a few lines of her own.

The aid-de-camp had taken his leave. Irma passed her hand over Walpurga's face and said: "Let me banish all your sad thoughts. Be happy and take my word for it--the man is saved. Go to the poor woman and quiet her in the mean while. I'll bring the answer to your room."

Walpurga could not find words, or she would have said something, even then. But the petition had already gone. After all no one would be harmed in the matter, and, although Thomas really was a wicked fellow, this might make a better man of him. Walpurga left Irma's apartment. Stopping at the door, for an instant, to recover herself, she heard Irma singing again. When she reached her room, she was in a calmer state and said to Zenza:

"Your Thomas will get off; depend upon it. But you must give me your word, and promise to keep it, too, that Thomas will become an honest man, and that you won't help him sell his stolen wares and hide his evil ways. You needn't look at me so, for I've a right to talk to you this way. I've risked a great deal for you."

"Yes, indeed; you've a right to say it," replied Zenza, in a half-earnest, half-jesting tone. "You make our whole neighborhood happy. We're all proud of you. On Sunday, before the church, I'll tell them what influence you have here, and they'll all believe me. Your mother was my playfellow, and if my Thomas had got an honest woman like you for his wife, he'd been thrifty, too. He must get himself a good wife. I'll give him no peace till he does."

Zenza was enjoying some good coffee which Mademoiselle Kramer had prepared for her, and the kind-hearted housekeeper filled her cup again and again.

"If I could only give my son some of this! Oh, how he must be suffering out there! But it serves him right; that's his punishment. He's on the lookout now, but not as a poacher. It's quite a different thing, now." Zenza was quite voluble and Mademoiselle Kramer was charmed with the frankness and motherly affection of the old woman.

When Zenza had emptied her cup and eaten nearly all the cake, she said:

"May I take this little bit of sugar with me? It'll always remind me that I've drunk coffee in the king's palace."

Mademoiselle Kramer wrapped a piece of cake in a paper, and said: "Take this to your son."

It seemed as though Zenza would never get done thanking them. She was in great good-humor, and asked permission to see the prince; but Walpurga refused it and well knew why; for, at home, Zenza was regarded as a witch and, even if it were mere superstition, thought Walpurga, who can know what might happen? She had already become so politic that she availed herself, as an excuse, of the doctor's order that no stranger should be allowed near the person of the crown prince.

Zenza now told them how great a commotion Walpurga's sudden departure had created in their neighborhood. Ever since, the people would talk of nothing else. The folks were all late at church on Sunday, because they had stopped before Walpurga's house and stared at it as if there was something new to be seen, and Hansei had been obliged to show his cow to half the congregation, as if there was something strange about it. But the thoughts of all were of Walpurga; and she also said that it was well known that Walpurga's influence had secured Stasi's betrothed his position as ranger. In spite of Walpurga's protestations that she knew nothing of it, Zenza insisted on her story, and praised her the more for her modesty.

The time passed quickly.

Countess Irma, her face radiant with joy, brought the king's letter of pardon.

Zenza would have fallen on her knees to her and kissed her feet, but Irma held her up and said:

"I've something more for you: take this, so that, besides being free, you may be able to get some pleasure."

She gave her a gold piece.

Old Zenza's eyes sparkled, while she said:

"If the gracious princess should ever want any one who'd go through fire and water to serve her, she need only think of Zenza and Thomas."

She would have said much more, but Walpurga said:

"Thomas is waiting for you at the gate; make haste and go to him."

"You see, dear princess, how good she is. She deserves to be happy."

"Walpurga," said Mademoiselle Kramer, "you might give the woman the money for your husband."

"I'll take it for you."

"No, I'll send it. I must wait awhile," said Walpurga hesitating. She could not well explain that she distrusted both Zenza and her son.

"Here," said Irma, handing Zenza the little golden heart which she wore; "take this to Walpurga's child, from me." Then, removing her silk kerchief, she added, "give her this, too."

"Oh, what a lovely neck!" exclaimed Zenza.

Walpurga again reminded her that she had better return to her son.

Irma felt happy to think that she had brought about the pardon. Walpurga was afraid to tell them Zenza was a stranger to her and that she almost hated her; or that Red Thomas was one of the worst men in their neighborhood. She consoled herself with the thought that all would yet be well. Bad men can grow better, or else all talk of repentance would be mere lies and deceit.

In the mean while, Zenza, holding the pardon on high, had hurried out of the palace.

"Is my reckoning settled?" asked Thomas, spitting as far as he could.

"Yes, thank God! See what a mother can do."

"I don't owe you much thanks for that, what did you bring me into the world for? But the best of it all is it's a slap in the face for the great snarling country justice. Now, mother, I'm as thirsty as three bailiff's clerks. Waiting has almost used me up. Have you anything more about you?"

"Of course I have; just look."

She showed him the gold piece, which he most dexterously removed from her hand and into his pocket.

"What else have you got?" said he, when he noticed the little gold heart that she had taken from her pocket at the same time.

"The beautiful princess gave me that and this silk kerchief for Walpurga's child."

"Hansei's child will have enough with the kerchief," said Thomas, appropriating the gold heart, while he good-naturedly allowed his mother to retain the black cord which had been attached to it.

"There, mother; that'll do very well, and now let's take a drink for having waited so long. While I was waiting out here, I saw a splendid rifle at the gunsmith's. You can take it apart and put it in your pocket, and we'll see if the greencoats catch me again."

The first thing young Thomas did was to take the chamois beard and the black cock plume out of his pocket and stick them in his hat again. Then he put on his hat in a defiant manner, and his whole bearing seemed to say: I'd like to see who'd dare touch them.

Just as they were going away, Baum came in from the street. He seemed anxious to avoid them, but Zenza went up to him and thanked him again for the handsome present he had given her when Walpurga had been sent for. She looked at him strangely and Baum, with a side glance, noticed that Thomas's eyes were fixed upon him. He felt a shudder passing like a flash of lightning, from his heart to his head. It actually made his hair stand on end, and obliged him to raise his hat and adjust it differently; but he took a nail-file from his pocket and began trimming his nails, and then said: "You've thanked me already; once is enough."

"Mother! if Jangerl wasn't in America, I'd have sworn that was he."

"You're crazy," replied Zenza.

They went into the town together. Thomas always walking briskly in front. It seemed as if it would not worry him much, were he to lose his mother.

They repaired to an inn, where, without taking time to sit down, he drank off a schoppen of wine. Then, telling his mother to wait, he went off to purchase the rifle.

Meanwhile, Walpurga was sitting by the window and imagining how the folks at home would be talking of her great power, and how, at the Chamois, they would have so much to say about her, and that the innkeeper's wife, who had always looked down upon her, would almost burst with envy.

Walpurga laughed and was pleased to think that the envious and proud would be angry at her good fortune. This, indeed, seemed her greatest delight, and at all events, was the thought on which she dwelt longest. Another reason may have been that the joy of the virtuous is more quickly exhausted than the angry and evil speeches of the wicked, which keep fermenting and sending bubbles to the surface long after they have been uttered. Walpurga remained sitting by the window, her lips silently moving, as if she were repeating to herself the words of those who envied and were angry at her, until, at last, Countess Irma addressed her:

"I can see how happy you are. Yes, Walpurga, if we could only do good to some fellow-creature every moment, we would be the happiest beings under the sun. Don't you see, Walpurga, the real divine grace of a prince lies in his being able to do good at any moment?"

"I understand that quite well," answered Walpurga. "A king is like the sun which shines down on all, and refreshes the trees near by, as well as the flowers in the distant, hidden valley; it does good to men and beast and everything. Such a king is a messenger from God; but he must be careful to remain one, for being lord over all pride and lust may overpower him. He's just given life to Thomas, and all the prison doors open as they do in the fable when they say: '*Open sesame,*' Oh, you good king! don't let them spoil you, and always have such kindhearted people about you as my Countess Irma."

"Thanks," said Irma. "I now know you perfectly. Believe me, all the books in the world contain nothing better and nothing more than does your heart; and, although you cannot write, it has been so much the more plainly written there.--But let us be quiet and sensible. Come, you must take your writing lesson."

They sat down together, and Irma taught Walpurga how to use the pen. Walpurga said that she did not care to write single letters, and that she would prefer having a word to copy.

Irma wrote the word "pardon" for her. Walpurga filled a whole sheet with that word, and when Irma left the room, she took the writing with her, saying:

"I shall preserve this as a memento of this hour."

CHAPTER III

"What can be the matter with the queen?--"

--"Her majesty," added Mademoiselle Kramer.

--"What can it be?" said Walpurga; "for some days, the prince--"

"His royal highness," said Mademoiselle Kramer.

--"Has hardly been noticed by her. Before that, whenever she saw the child and held it to her heart, she always seemed lifted up to the skies, and once said to me: 'Walpurga, didn't it make you feel as if you'd become a girl again, free and independent of everything? To me, the world is nothing but myself and my child'--and now she hardly looks at it, just as if her having had a child were a dream. There must be great trouble in a mother's heart--"

"Royal mother," said Mademoiselle Kramer.

--"When she doesn't care to look at her child."

The queen's heart was, in truth, torn by a mighty struggle.

Her feelings had, for months past, been of a most distressing and excited nature. There was one point on which she dared not even think aloud, and which she would have thought profaned by speaking of it to others. It was her wish to determine for herself, and she had done so. Ever since she had become a mother, she had felt as if separated from the rest of the world. When she thought of her child and, above all, when she clasped it to her heart, she felt as if nothing more remained to be done. She and the child were her world; all else was as nothing. And yet she loved the king with all her heart, and ardently desired that their union should be so complete that they be one in feeling, in belief, and in affection.

The thought that they ought to be united in all things, constantly grew upon her. Father, mother and child should be as one, praying to the same God, with the same thoughts, and in the same words.

The isolation of the sick chamber only helped to strengthen these thoughts, and, now that she was about to return to the world, she longed to make the bond that united her to the king, perfect in the highest sense.

She was allowed to do but little talking, and, therefore, did not indulge in conversation. After a few days had passed, she had a Madonna, by Filippo Lippi the younger, brought to her dimly lighted chamber. She gazed at the picture for hours, and it seemed to be looking at her in return--the two mothers were one in bliss.

The canon visited her and found her in this devotional frame of mind. With trembling lips, she confided to him her desire to belong to the church of her husband and child. He lent a ready assent to the request that she might be spared all dogmatic teachings. When the canon had left, she became oppressed with a sense of fear. There goes a man, thought she, who bears my secret with him. He had promised to keep it to himself and thus prove himself worthy her confidence. But the secret had, nevertheless, ceased to be entirely her own.

She soon quieted her fears, and a glow of delight overspread her features at the thought that, although she was now a mother, there was yet another sublime and exalted function which would perfect her union with her husband and furnish one more proof of her great love for him.

In the fullness of life, the thought of death occurred to her, and she ordered another painting to be placed on the easel before her. It was the Maria Ægyptica, by Ribera.

The queen often felt as if she must seek the glance of the penitent. But those eyes, instead of beholding aught, seem as if listening: not in alarm, for an angel is calling to her--but submissive and trustful, for she is used to the sound of heavenly voices. Instead of representing the penitent daughter of the king as crushed and bruised from having mortified the flesh, the artist has made her features expressive of restored, childlike innocence and youthful beauty--a nude figure, divested of all raiment, wrapped in the long, fair tresses that descend to her knees. She is kneeling beside the open grave that is to receive her. Her blue eyes gaze into eternity; her lips are closed, as if in pain, and above her hovers an angel who spreads the mantle of mercy over her and exclaims: "Thou art forgiven!" Forgiven and redeemed, she sinks into the grave.

The ascetic tone of the picture fully accorded with the queen's mood, and the canon often found her lost in ecstatic admiration of it.

Although Doctor Gunther disapproved of this mute companionship, his wishes and his orders were alike unavailing. It was the first time that this man, who was so highly esteemed by the queen, had encountered obstinacy and unyielding defiance at her hands. When Irma saw the picture, she carelessly remarked that the position of the eyes was faulty, but that the artist had skillfully availed himself of this fault in order to produce a peculiar expression. The queen pressed her hand to her heart--she was alone in her feelings and wished to remain so.

Walpurga was successful where both Gunther and Irma had failed.

"Is that a forest-sprite?" asked she,

"What's that?"

"Out our way, they tell of the forest-sprites. They haunt the mountains on ghost-nights, and can wrap themselves in their long hair."

The queen related the legend of Maria Ægyptica to Walpurga. She was a princess who had led a dissolute life. Suddenly, she left the palace and, renouncing all pleasures, went out into the desert, where she supported herself on roots and lived many years, until all her clothes fell from her body: and, when her dying hour arrived, an angel descended from above and spread the mantle of mercy over her--

"That's all very good and pretty," said Walpurga, "but, no offense to you, my queen, it seems a sin to have such a terrible picture before one's eyes. I wouldn't want to sleep in the same room with it. It seems as if some night it would come down and drag me into the open grave with it. Oh, dear Lord! I'm afraid of it, even in broad daylight."

Walpurga's words were not without effect. When night came, the queen really imagined that the picture was coming toward her. She could not sleep, and was obliged to have it removed during the night.

Her calmness and equanimity were thus restored, and, as reading was now permitted her, the priest provided her with suitable books.

Her whole life was possessed by the one idea. Walpurga had observed correctly. The queen scarcely looked at her child, although the step she contemplated taking was prompted by love for her husband and her child.

A few days before she went out for the first time, she sent for the king, and said:

"Kurt, next Sunday will be the first time that I go out, and the first day that I enter your church, and that of our son. Henceforth, I shall pray at the same altar with you and him."

"I don't understand you--"

"I have vowed that if God, in his mercy, would preserve my life and that of the child, I would be united with you in all things. I am not fulfilling an enforced vow, but a free and well-considered resolution. I offer this, not as a new proof, but rather as a confirmation or final sealing of our love. Kurt, my every thought, all that I am, is yours. We are as one before the world; let us be as one before God. Henceforth, we will not take separate ways, or have separate thoughts. Let our child learn nothing of the differences between men, and, above all, between those to whom he owes his life. I feel happy that I can do this as a free offering and not as a sacrifice."

"Mathilde," said the king, with a strangely cold tone, "is this the first time you speak of this, or have you already made preparations--"

"My resolution was formed in secret, and in all earnestness. Afterward, I announced it and all is now in readiness. I had intended it as a surprise for you. The canon almost insisted that I must tell you of it in his presence, but I wouldn't consent."

"Thank God!" said the king, drawing a long breath, "all may again be well!"

"'Again?' 'Well?'" inquired the queen in amazement.

The king calmly explained to her that, although he appreciated the sacrifice, he could not accept it. The queen deprecated his terming it a sacrifice, and the king said:

"Very well, then; you need go no further than myself, who of all beings am most in accord with you, to discover that others may--nay, must--judge of your actions differently from yourself. What will the world, the courts, our subjects, think of it?"

"What need we care about that, when we know that we are right? 'What will the world say?' is always the great question. But the world must not force us to be different from what we are."

"Mathilde, you speak like a martyr. Your feelings are exalted and worthy of all reverence. You are both good and noble; but, believe me, the best actions, indeed, the only proper ones, are those which require neither explanations nor apology. We are not hermits. Although your motives are pure and lofty, the world will be unable and unwilling to understand them. Nor dare we make explanations. A prince degrades himself by stooping to explain his actions. You regard the world with heavenly feelings; but the heaven lies in your way of looking at things, not in the world itself. I should be sorry to reveal the world's wickedness to you, and thus cast a gloom over your kindly views of life. Hold fast to your belief in the Highest, but do it after the forms of your own faith."

"And must I, all my life, walk in one path, while you and the child take another?"

"Mathilde, we are not anchorites; we are not even private citizens. Our position is an exposed one. A sovereign can have no private actions--"

"Do you mean that all we do is to be as an example to others?"

"I mean that, too," said the king, hesitating; "but what I meant to say was, that, in whatever you do, it is not yourself alone, but the queen who acts. Its effects are felt far and near. I am happy to be the object of so much love. You feel it, do you not, Mathilde?"

"Don't speak of it. Our best and deepest feelings do not seek expression in words."

"Bear this well in mind--the wife of a private gentleman can perform such an action in secret. You cannot. You would be obliged to close the Protestant court chapel, and would thus offend all throughout the land who hold your present faith."

"I don't wish to offend any one. The world can't ask me to make such a sacrifice. My highest, my only aim, is to be one with you, on earth and in heaven, now and hereafter."

"Very well, then; promise me one thing."

"Whatever you wish."

"Promise me that you will defer acting on your resolve, for at least a month. It would be wrong to allow a passing mood to change the course of one's life."

"You're a noble creature," said the queen; "I'll obey you."

"So you give up your resolve?"

"No, I shall wait. I don't wish it to be what you imagine it--the outgrowth of a sickly mood, engendered by the seclusion of my chamber. I'll allow it to ripen in the sunlight, and you will then discover that it is something more than a mere mood."

The king was satisfied with the result. But, strangely enough, he refrained from any display of affection, and when, at parting, he took the queen's hand in his, his manner seemed cold and distant.

CHAPTER IV

The king had shown great self-command while conversing with his wife, and, now that he was alone, felt that her words had aroused a dormant feeling of displeasure.

He sincerely loved his wife, but he was of an heroic, active temperament, and all that savored of pettiness, self-questioning or sentimentality, was utterly distasteful to him. His great ambition was to promote the happiness of his subjects, and to achieve for himself a place in history. But a period of peaceful development, in which all were friendly to the government and anxious to serve it, afforded no opportunity for heroic deeds, or for new and startling measures. All that could be done was to hold fast to what had already been achieved and, at the same time, to encourage new growths. But such labors absorb the work of many whose names remain unknown to fame, and it was this that explained the king's fondness for building. The construction of great edifices devoted to art, science, the church and the army, could not but be regarded as proofs of a mind anxious to achieve great deeds.

The king loved his wife, and was content to have it so. The queen, on the other hand, was ever anxious to furnish new proofs of her love, and her deep sensibility was again displayed in this attempt to carry out a resolve which, although prompted by the best motives, was utterly impracticable. She idealized everything, and, in that respect, the king's temperament was the very opposite of hers. Her apartments were always so dimly lighted that, when he entered them, he was obliged to grope his way. On emerging from this gloom, it seemed to him as if the morn had dawned anew, for he dearly loved the bright light of day. This continual worrying about religious problems that none can solve--this constant mental excitement, incapacitates one for prompt action. He who desires to have his life-fabric rest on a firm foundation, must be free from over-refined self-criticism. He must subordinate all his feelings, all his passions, to the one aim, and to no one does this so forcibly apply as to the monarch who desires to direct the diversified and all-embracing interests of his subjects.

The queen's aim was to realize, in her own person, her ideal of the wife and the mother; but then she had no right to forget that she was a queen. Something more was required than eternal trifling and weaving of garlands, ingeniously devised as they might be. Love, such as hers, is exacting withal, for, while it lavishes endearments, it constantly requires a return in kind. It is exclusive and, at the same time, wearisome. The sun shines and love exists, but why constantly worry about either.

The lonely life the queen had been leading had produced an excited condition that sought vent in the attempt to change her faith, and, although the king had determined that it should be nothing more than an attempt, her words had tended to confirm a corresponding feeling of loneliness on his part--a result to which his recent experience had in no slight degree contributed.

The king was alone in his cabinet. How would it have stood with him, if his wife had possessed a great and commanding mind? The thought had suddenly flashed upon him. He passed his hand across his brow, as if to banish the idea; he dared not, could not think of such a thing. He sent for Doctor Gunther, for this affair must be disposed of at once.

Gunther came.

The king, at first, cautiously sounded him, in order to discover whether this confidant of the queen's knew aught of what had happened, and then, under the seal of secrecy, informed him of all.

To the king's great surprise, Gunther, instead of thanking him for this mark of confidence, politely said:

"I should much prefer that Your Majesty had graciously permitted me to remain ignorant of secrets and troubles in which I can be of no assistance."

The king stared at him in astonishment. This man was always obstinate and preserved his dignity.

"I was about to ask you," said the king, harshly, "whether you believe that you can influence the queen in this matter."

"I fear not; but if Your Majesty desires it, I am ready to make the effort."

"Pray do."

"But I fear her majesty will be offended. I understand her idiosyncrasies. If the matter is noised about, she will think it profaned by the touch of others, and it will thus, in her opinion, lose its greatest charm."

"That would be the very thing," said the king, eagerly. "Perhaps that will be the best way to cure her of her enthusiasm. Everything is considered a fit subject for debate, nowadays. Your friends in the chamber of delegates debate everything, and they might as well--"

It was a constant source of annoyance to the king, that the doctor, who never obtruded his opinions, would, when drawn into an argument on questions of religion or politics, always espouse the liberal side; but, with all that, he could ill afford to do without Gunther. Although the king found him objectionable in some respects, he nevertheless had a high regard for him. He held so high a position in the world of science and in the esteem of his countrymen, that the presence, near the king, of one possessed of such liberal views, reflected peculiar glory on the court itself.

The king now formally requested Gunther to endeavor to move the queen from her resolve.

It was a difficult undertaking.

The queen had, heretofore, made this trusted friend her confidant, and now he was possessed of a secret of hers that had been given him by another. Gunther endeavored to draw the queen into some allusion to her secret resolve, but, failing in the attempt, was obliged to introduce the subject himself.

The queen seemed surprised and grieved.

"Why has the king done this?" asked she, her features expressing intense pain.

"Perhaps his majesty," replied Gunther, "credits me with the possession of more powerful arguments that any which have yet been advanced."

"I know them, all," answered the queen, excitedly; "in such a matter, no stranger should dare to breathe a word of--"

"Then, Your Majesty, I've nothing more to say, and humbly beg leave to withdraw."

"No, no! Speak on--I must hear you."

"Must? You must not."

"Wish, or must, it's all the same. You're always saying that there's no such thing as free will, and with monarchs it is certainly so."

"Your Majesty," said Gunther, in a gentle voice, "the high resolve you have formed was not an act of your will. It is the natural and inevitable consequence of a chain of events and impressions, which have been shaped by your temperament. Fervent natures are always afraid lest they cannot do enough for themselves and for the world. They would like, with every hour--nay, with every breath--to make others happy, or impress the world with some great thought."

"So you, too, can flatter."

"I never flatter. I simply take the diagnosis which, in your case, is not flattering. This excess of sensibility is not health--"

"So you consider my mood as unhealthy--"

"We should not use that term.--But I entreat you. Your Majesty! this tone, with either of us, is hardly--"

"Speak on. I like to hear you. I don't feel hurt that you know of this. I regard you as part of the daylight that was to ripen my resolve."

"Well then, all that is to ripen must needs be subjected to currents of air and even to storms. But I shall bring you no storm, and shall not even speak of the fact that whoever deserts the faith into which he was born, insults his parents; nor shall I tell you that the ceremonies to which we have been accustomed from youth, are the soul's mother-tongue. All that does not address itself to the mind. Mind and reason are the parents of conscious man. It is our duty to live up to our convictions, and I can, therefore, find no fault with a change of religion based upon conviction. But it seems to me, Your Majesty, that your change of faith is simply superficial or, if it be deeper, only from love for your husband. You know, however, that I view all these things from an entirely different standpoint. I believe I know the spring in paradise, whence flows the stream that on earth is divided into so many little rivulets; and these again, to use the words of my friend Eberhard, Countess Irma's father, furnish the power for the mills that grind out sermons. Your Majesty knows that the legend of the four streams that flowed from the tree Igdrasil, which is found in the most beautiful of all books, the Bible, is also to be found in our old German Saga."

"Very well--but I beg of you, my dear friend, spare me your literary curiosities."

"Your Majesty," resumed Gunther, "as long as we remain in the faith of our fathers, we can enjoy great latitude of opinion. Our thoughts can reach far beyond its confines, and no inquisition has power over us: but, as soon as we profess another religion, we forfeit the right to be free. It is our duty to live up to it. One who is noble by birth can afford to admit civil equality, but he who has had nobility conferred on him, cannot do so. Will Your Majesty permit me to say one word more? I regard it as fortunate for mankind in general, and our German fatherland in particular, that there is a diversity of religious beliefs. That of itself tends to preserve feelings of humanity, for thus we cannot help seeing that there are different forms of soul utterances for one and the same thing. A multiplicity of sects affords the best protection against fanaticism and, moreover, helps to prove that religious forms are of no consequence; that is, one can be righteous in any faith and, indeed, without any outward show of religion."

Gunther remained with the queen for a long while, offering further explanations of the ideas he had advanced.

He was still with her, when the canon was announced.

The queen sent word that she desired to be excused, and requested him to come the next day.

When Gunther left, she was still as firm in her resolve as at first. She felt persuaded that this was an action in which no other being should interfere, and, least of all, a man.

She was on the point of taking Irma into her confidence. She felt that the countess was clever and, moreover, a true friend. Unconquerable dread held her back. She feared lest she might appear weak and vacillating in Irma's eyes.

CHAPTER V

For days, the queen remained alone. Walpurga and the child were the only ones permitted near her. She did not wish to speak to any one else, be it her husband, Gunther, or the priest.

One afternoon, when Walpurga was with her, she felt impelled to ask:

"Walpurga, do you know that I don't belong to your faith?"

"Yes, indeed, I do; and I'm glad of it."

"Glad of it?"

"Of course I am; you're the first and only Lutheran I've ever known, and if they're all like you, it must be a beautiful religion."

"It is beautiful, and so are all religions that make good beings of us."

"Why, do you know, queen, that's the very thing my father used to say, and in the very same words? Oh, if he'd only lived long enough to have had a talk with you."

The queen was silent for a long while.

At last she asked:

"Walpurga, if your religion was different from Hansei's, would you go to his church?"

"Why, Hansei's Catholic, as well as I am."

"But if it were otherwise?"

"But it isn't otherwise."

"But just imagine it were."

"But I can't do that," said she, as if about to cry.

The queen was again silent for some time. Presently Walpurga, of her own accord, said:

"Yes, I can, after all. I've thought it out. Why, you're Lutheran and your husband's Catholic. But why do you ask me that?"

"Imagine yourself in my position. If you were a Protestant, would you not visit your husband's church?"

"No, queen, never! As long as I'd been an honest wife while a Protestant, I'd remain one. May I tell you a little story, queen?"

"Yes; go on."

"What was I going to say?--Yes, now I know.--You see, my dear father--the king's physician has surely told you what a good man he was--But I'm beginning at the wrong end; I wanted to tell it to you differently.--Well, as I was going to say, I went to school to a very strict priest who condemned all people that didn't belong to our faith, to the lowest depths of hell. I was once telling my father about it, when he said: 'Purgei,'--he always called me Purgei when he wanted to speak right to my heart--'Purgei,' said he, 'there are many millions of people in the world, and the smallest portion of them are Christians, and what a vile God it would be who would condemn all the rest to hell just because they aren't Christians, when they can't help it, and were born as they are. Don't you believe,' said he, 'that a man's damned for his faith; as long as he's virtuous.' Well, I hold fast by that. Of course, I didn't say anything to the priest about it, for he needn't know everything. I'm sure he don't tell me all he knows."

The queen was silent, and Walpurga soon began again:

"And now I think of something, better than all. Oh, my dear queen, I must tell you this, too. It's about my father, who used to think a great deal. The old doctor, the father of the one who's living there now, often used to say that if father had studied he'd have become a great man. Well, one evening, on the very Sunday that I was confirmed, I was sitting with father and mother on the bench behind our little cottage by the lake. The evening bells were tolling; we had said our aves and were sitting about in front of the cottage, when we heard the Liederkranz. They were coming across the lake in a boat, and were singing so beautifully--I can't tell you how lovely their singing was. And then father got up from his seat, his face glowing in the sunshine, and said: 'Now I know how our Lord in heaven must feel.' 'Don't blaspheme,' said my mother. 'I'm not blaspheming; quite the reverse,' said father. His voice seemed wondrous strange. 'Yes, I know it, I feel it,' said he; 'all churches--our own, the Protestant, the Jewish, the Turkish, and whatever their names may be--every one of them has a part in the song, and though each sings as best he can, they go together very well, and make a chorus that must sound glorious up there in heaven. Let every one sing according to the voice God has given him, for He will know how it will harmonize, and it surely does harmonize beautifully.'"

Walpurga's beaming glance met that of the queen.

"Your father spoke wisely," said the queen; a tear glistened in her eye and in that of the nurse, too.

Walpurga went away, taking the child with her.

The next day the queen sent for the king, and said:

"Kurt, I have courage."

"I know it."

"No. I have a courage that you do not know."

"A courage that I do not know?"

"And never will know. I have courage enough to appear weak and vacillating; but, Kurt, you will not misjudge me on that account?"

"Pray speak more plainly, and with fewer preliminaries."

"I am determined," continued the queen, "I hardly dare utter that word, now--but you will not misjudge me? I shall remain in the faith in which I was born, and we shall nevertheless be as one."

The king thanked her quite cordially, and only regretted that the canon knew of the matter. He hoped, however, to be able to silence his tongue.

The queen was surprised to find that he manifested so little joy; but, on second thought, this seemed quite natural to her, for why should that which had been nothing more than a passing cloud, leave great results in its wake? Others could know nothing of the bitter struggle it had cost her.

She felt sensible that it would be a long while before any expression or resolve of hers would obtain weight or authority, for it would not soon be forgotten that she had once shown herself weak.

While she was in the Protestant court chapel, on the following Sunday, she scarcely ventured to raise her eyes. She was thinking of how it would have been if she now were in the other church, and of how the eyes of the congregation would have been directed to the pew that was thenceforward to remain vacant. In spirit, she had already deserted this church and its congregation. Her soul trembled when she thought of the resolve she had entertained, and, from the bottom of her heart, she thanked her husband, whose strong arm had held her back.

When the whole congregation arose and, in the prayers for the royal household, offered up thanks for her preservation and that of the royal prince, she could no longer restrain her tears.

Contrary to her usual habit, she went to church again that afternoon.

Meanwhile, the king and Countess Irma were pleasantly sauntering in that portion of the park from which the public was shut out.

The king informed Irma of the queen's resolve and of how she had been induced to give it up. Irma replied that she had, long since, surmised as much, but had not felt that she had a right to speak of it. She had dropped a hint to Doctor Gunther, who had refused to have anything to do with the matter.

The king expressed his dislike for Gunther, but Irma defended him with great enthusiasm.

"The doctor is very fortunate," said the king, "to have so eloquent an advocate in his absence."

"I am that to all friends whom I truly respect."

"I could wish that I, too, were accused," continued the king.

"And I believe," replied Irma, smiling, "Your Majesty could not wish for a more earnest advocate than I would be."

A pause ensued. The king gracefully and frankly retracted his complaints against Gunther, and this conversation seemed merely a bridge over which they passed to another topic.

The king spoke of the queen and of her peculiar temperament.

It was the first time that the king and Irma had spoken of the queen. That the king not only prompted, but actually called forth her remarks, was the cause, at a later day, of incalculable suffering.

They extolled the poetic sense, the fervent feeling, the flower-like tenderness of the queen, and while they thus depicted her in glowing colors, they, in their own minds, found fault with her weakness and overflowing enthusiasm.

When a husband thus speaks of his wife, to a third person, it inevitably leads to estrangement and exposure.

Thus far, all was veiled in terms of praise. It was here just as it was with the queen in church. With all the power of her will, she strove to forget herself in her prayer, and to be again as she had once been; and yet, while the sense of the words she uttered entered her soul, she could not help being aware of a secret numbness and estrangement that seemed to say to her: "You will never again be as you once were."

While the king and Irma were thus conversing, they appeared to each other as equals. Their views of life were in accord, and while they spoke of how easily one might yield to temptation, their intimacy seemed to them a proof of strength rather than of weakness. They went on in perfect step with each other, and Irma no longer said: "Let us return."

The queen, since she had again appeared in society, was, if possible, more gracious and amiable than she had ever been. She placed every one far above her. They had none of them been as weak and vacillating as she. She felt it her duty to do good to every one, because, although she was no better than they, she was placed far above them. Her soul was all humility.

A few days later, the newspapers mysteriously hinted that attempts had been made to take advantage of the angelic purity of the queen, in order to estrange her from herself and alienate the affections of the people from her.

This, it was readily understood, alluded to the queen's contemplated change of faith.

The queen had always openly acknowledged herself on the side of the liberal opposition, and the king regarded Gunther as the mediator who had procured her the goodwill of the press, and who, in doing so, had not feared committing an indiscretion.

This plain and flagrant perversion of the truth only served the more to embitter him against the press and the machinations of the queen's party at court. Nevertheless, he dissembled his resentment, for he felt that he could well afford to bide his time.

CHAPTER VI

(IRMA TO HER FRIEND EMMA)

"Let me tell you all that I did yesterday. I wanted to read--I saw the letters but could not read a word, for they all seemed to be moving about the page, like so many ants in an anthill. I wanted to sing, but no song was to my liking. I wanted to play, but even Beethoven seemed strange, and I lay for hours, dreaming. I followed the little mother and her son beyond the mountain. The larks sang my thoughts to them. They reach their home, and the wild, daring lad is tractable once more. He carols his merry song to his beloved. I fancy I hear him. Ah, Emma! what is there so glorious as making others happy? It is hard enough to be a human being, fettered by a thousand trammels, by ailments, consideration for others, and all sorts of misery; but to suffer want beside! The very idea of jails is a disgrace to humanity. Ah, Emma! how noble, how like a revelation from the great heart of the people, were the words of the simple-minded wife of the wood-cutter. I tried to put what she had said into verse, intending to give it to the king the next morning; but I could not do it; nothing satisfied me. Language is worn out, narrow, coarse. I was ever thinking of Schiller's words: 'When the soul speaks, it has ceased to be the soul.' I left my scribbling. I passed a restless night. When the soul's depths are stirred, it wanders about like a spirit, and can find no rest in sleep.

"While at breakfast this morning, I informed the king of what Walpurga had said. I was annoyed to find that he did not understand more than half of it. How else could he have answered me: 'Yes, the Highlanders have great affection for their rulers. Pray tell that to your father.'

"The king observed that he had made a mistake, but, adroit and amiable as he is, quickly recovered his good nature and said: 'Dear Countess, I will give you a secret title, which is to be known only by us two. I appoint you as spy on the popular heart. Seek and listen, and whenever you find anything, you can always count upon unquestioning compliance on my part. Does it not seem to you that Egeria was nothing more than a spy on the popular heart? At the altar in the temple, she could overhear the secret thoughts of the people, and then repeated them to king Numa, whom they deified and adored.'

"'But our people only use prescribed prayers,' said I.

"'The thought is quite suggestive,' replied the king, and when Schnabelsdorf entered shortly afterward, he commissioned him to make brief notes of what fixed prayers the Grecians and Romans used in their temples.

"And thus the whole story ended. What I had imagined would create a deep impression, merely served to furnish amusement for an evening.

"Ah, dear Emma, *amusement* is the point about which all revolves. If an apostle were to appear to-day, he could not help preaching, 'Ask not, how shall we amuse ourselves to-day, but'--etc., etc.,--finish the sentence for yourself.

"I am no better than the rest of them. I, too, am nothing but a puppet, wound up to run seventy years, and to dance and laugh and ride and amuse itself in the mean while. All of us are mere singing-birds; the only difference being that some are contented with grain and caterpillars and flies, while others require larger morsels, such as rabbits, bucks, deer, pheasants, fish. And the higher education of that variety of singing-birds known as man, lies in the fact that he cooks his food. There is terrible vacuity in many men. *To make conversation.* Therein lies the whole art. Try to get a clear notion of the expression: *to make conversation*, and you will find how nonsensical it is. The people find me entertaining, but I don't *make* conversation. I merely speak when I have somewhat to say.

"My evil spirit is constantly shouting the word '*dilettante*' in my ear.

"'Dilettante--One who junkets or feeds on tit-bits for pastime,'--says my dictionary. Rather rough, but there is something in it."

"One day later.

"The king has just sent me the following poem. I must apologize to him; he seems to have understood my communication far better than I had suspected. What do you think of the lines? Why should a king not write verses? Ideality is required of him. Indeed a king should understand all things, but be a dilettante in none.

"P. S.--I have just looked at the lines again, and find that I cannot copy them for you."

"A day later.

"Don't laugh at my continually telling you of Walpurga.

"It was during our writing-lesson to-day, that the king found me with her. He told me how much pleasure it had afforded him to be able to pardon her relative.

"'Our relationship is very distant,' said she, 'nothing more than forty-second cousins; and, Your Majesty, I've something on my mind. If Red Thomas turns out badly, I can't help it.'

"The king laughed and replied: 'Nor can I.' It is hard to understand how Walpurga never speaks of Zenza and her son except in anger, and that she will have nothing to do with them. Strange demons jostle each other in the hearts of the people. I fear that my office of spy on the popular heart will prove very difficult.

"By the king's orders, I have been furnished with a copy of the church prayers of the Greeks and Romans.

"I must write it down and then the idea will cease tormenting me. I am constantly picturing to myself, how would it have been if Zenza had become first lady of the bedchamber, and her son, the poacher, master of the hounds. She would be ready enough of speech. She has exceedingly clever and cunning eyes, and the lad would surely have been an elegant cavalier.

"In spite of all their prating about human equality and pride of birth, I cannot help regarding it as a sign of divine grace, that I was born a countess, instead of Zenza's daughter; but there are two sides to that question.

"God's creatures are not so badly off in this world, after all. The frog croaking in the marsh is just as happy as the nightingale that sings on the tree.

"To say to the frog, 'Thou, too, should'st dwell in the rosebush and sing like the nightingale,' were not humane, but simply tyrannical.

"Have you ever patiently listened to the croaking of the frogs? How expressive it is of comfort! While I write, they are having a grand concert over in the park pond. I enjoy listening to them. We human beings are impudent enough to judge everything by the standard of our own taste, and yet Mistress Frog will, very justly, find no music so sweet to her ears as the song of Master Frog.

"I feel so grateful, dear Emma, that I can write everything to you. You cannot imagine what a relief it is to me.

"I am a spy on my own heart; there are many wild spirits in it--adventurers and fortune-hunters and, with them all, a nun. I am quite curious to know how so mixed a company will get on together.

"My behavior toward the whole court is so free and independent, because I have a secret daily task: writing to you.

"But my thoughts go out to you a thousand times oftener:

There's not an hour in the silent night.
But what my thoughts go out to thee.

"Do you remember it? It was your favorite song. I sing it, for your sake, at least once every day. You and my piano are all in all to me. You patiently await my coming. All the music of all the masters that ever were. Or ever will be, dwells within you, and you only await the coming of the one whose touch can release those tones.

"I have a dual soul. In its one phase, the piano--in its other, the zither. The one is easily moved from place to place; the other not. The one requires that the fingers touch the strings. But ah, dear Emma, I scarce know what I am writing. I wish I could get rid of the habit of thinking. I wish I were Zenza's daughter and the poacher were my brother. But no; our thieves and rogues who have been at school long enough to know the seven cardinal sins and the whole of the catechism by heart, are timid and cowardly; they drop the petition for pardon into their mother's lap, while they stand by whining: Forgive us, we have done nothing wrong. All the world over, there is no longer genuine scorn of nature. Methinks the 'Italian robber behind the rock' that you once worked in wools, has, in these days, ceased to be more than a traditional pattern for embroidery. The arts simply serve to gloss over life.

"Good-night--good-night."

"A day later,

"I never read what I have once written. I do not care to be reminded of it again. Yesterday's sun does not shine to-day.--But that was not what I meant. The sun is the same, but the light is ever new, and I am happy to-day and do not care for all the churches and palaces, men and women, frogs and crocodiles in the world.

"To-day, the king said to me:

"'I am well aware, Countess, that you have thought contemptuously of me, during the last two days. Every withdrawal of your sympathy affects me as sensibly as if it were an electric shock. Do not let this happen again, I beg of you!' and while he spoke, he looked at me like a beseeching child. Ah, he has such deep, beautiful eyes!

"I remember your once saying to me: 'There are glances without a background, void of depth or soul'; but the glances of this friend have unfathomed depths.

"The bonds that held me captive shall no longer restrain me! I--I--but no--I cannot write the word.

"Oh, Emma! How I wish I were a peasant on a lonely mountain height. Last night, it seemed to me as if my native mountains were calling out to me, 'Come home'--'Do come'--'It is good to be with us.' Ah, I would like to come, but cannot.

"Walpurga is a great friend to me at present. I become absorbed in her life, so full of true, natural repose. I find it excessively amusing to behold the court as reflected through her eyes. It seems like a very puppet-play, and we, like two merry children at a raree-show.

"We often sing together, and I have learned some lovely songs from her. Oh, how charmingly independent the country people are.

"'On mountain heights there dwells no sin.' The song is ever haunting me.

"The king departs for the baths to-day: my brother is in his suite. The king requested me to write to him, now and then. I shall not do it."

"Two days later,

"The king knows that I cannot live unless there be flowers in my room, and has given orders to have a fresh bouquet placed there every day. This displeases me. A flower that a friend has stooped to pluck for you is worth more than a thousand artistically arranged bouquets.

"The king has also left orders that bouquets shall be sent daily to Baroness N---- and Countess A----. I think this is only to avoid remarks upon the attentions shown me. I am angry at the king. He shall not have a line from me.

"I have for some time past been taking lessons in modeling, from a professor at the academy. He has finished a bust of me, and has used it as a model for a figure of Victory, to be placed on the new arsenal. Have I not reason to be proud? After this, I shall ever be in the open air, and shall see nothing but the blue sky, the sun, the moon, and the stars, and, at noon, the guard-mounting.

"The professor says that I have talent for modeling. This has made me quite happy. Painting and drawing are only half the battle--mere makeshifts. Will you permit me, on my return, to make a *relievo* of you?

"Did I not, in one of my letters to you, speak of a secret in regard to the queen?

"I think I did.

"The affair is now at an end. For love of the king, the queen wished to enter our church, or rather yours--pardon me, once and for all time, I have no church. The king behaved nobly in the matter. I shall never forget the time he told me of it. He is, indeed, a great man. How glorious it is, that there are princes on earth who realize our ideal of the perfect man. Free and yet self-possessed, unspoiled, unperverted and unbiased. If there were no kings, we could no longer know a free, beautiful, perfect man. I use the word *beautiful* in its highest sense, and of course presuppose the existence of a noble mind. All are not gods who suffer themselves to be worshiped.

"The poet and the king are, of all men, alone perfect. All others--be they musicians or painters, sculptors or architects, artists or scholars--have narrow, contracted vocations, solo instruments, as it were. The poet and the king are the only ones who grasp life in all its phases. To them, naught is devoid of meaning, because all belongs to them. The poet creates a world; the king is a world in himself. The poet knows and depicts the shepherd and the huntsman, the king and the waiting-maid, the seamstress--in fact, all. But the king is hunter and statesman, soldier and farmer, scholar and artist, all in himself. He represents the orchestra of talents. Thus is he king, and thus does he represent a people, an age--aye, humanity itself, and at its best.

"Ah, Emma! Call me Turandot. Schoning, the poetic chamberlain, is also paying his addresses to me.

"Do you know what I ought to have been?

"I do.

"Queen of a tribe of savages. That is what I was created for. My true vocation would be to found a new civilization. Don't laugh at me. I am not joking; indeed, I'm not. I am fit for something far better than all I have here. I am not modest. I judge others and myself, too. I know my merits and my faults, also.

"On father's estate, there is a hammock that hangs between two elms. My greatest pleasure was to lie in it, suspended in the air, while I dreamt of distant woods.

"Do you know some savage tribe that would elect me as its queen? I have procured some of the Indian melodies, if they really deserve the name. One of the professors at the university, who spent six years among the Indians, recently gave a lecture at court. He brought some of their instruments with him, and had them played on. There was more noise than music. It seemed like the lisping of a nation which, as regards civilization, is yet in its infancy."

"Four o'clock in the morning,

"Forget all that I have written to you, as you would the breezes and the weather-changes of yesterday.

"I have just left my bed, in order to write to you. I cannot sleep. I am scarcely dressed while I sit here speaking to you. Oh, that I *could* speak to you! Writing is a miserable makeshift--nay, helplessness itself.

"I don't know what ails me. All that I am--my very self--seems as if only for the time being. I feel as if waiting for something, I know not what. I fancy that the very next moment must bring it, and that I shall either be doing some wonderful thing, or have it happen to me--that I shall be completely changed and become a great healing power, instead of the puny, useless child of man that I now am. I listen and fancy that I must hear a tone that has never yet been uttered on earth.

"There is no use trying--I cannot write. I imagined that it would soothe me if I could force myself to think and speak of all things in definite terms, but I know nothing definite. I only know that I am unhappy. Not unhappy, but as if dead and yet alive. I imagine myself a sleep-walker.

"I can write no more. I close my letter and shall go to bed. I want to sleep. All the world about me lies hushed in slumber. Oh, that I could dream myself into another world, even though my sleep were one from which there is no waking!

"Good-night! Good-morning!
IRMA."

CHAPTER VII

"To-morrow, I mean to bring Countess Irma to you," said Doctor Gunther to his wife, one evening. "She's the daughter of my old friend."

"In voice and manner, the countess is full of majesty, but her singing is not practical."

"Then you shall teach her. She will be glad to learn from you."

"If she be willing, I am quite at her service."

The doctor was delighted to find it so easy to bring the two ladies together. He knew, of course, that his wife complied with his every wish, but in this instance he was doubly anxious that all should go smoothly.

For some time past, he had observed that Irma was in a feverish condition which, during the last few days, had been growing worse; but he was one of those physicians who pay great attention to mental conditions and, instead of waiting for disease to make its appearance, endeavor to avert it by proper changes in the mode of living. He did not know the cause of Irma's excitement, but he knew that her temperament was one of extremes, and felt sure that if she could only obtain an insight into a pure home and, perhaps, become initiated into its ways, it would have a tranquilizing effect and lead her mind to move in quieter channels. He had enough experience to know that there are no substitutes for sympathy and friendship, but felt that the acquaintance of a citizen's wife, of exalted character and ripe culture, could not fail to have an effect upon Irma, who had thus far known no life but that of the cloister and the court.

Gunther had no need to give his wife instructions, or even a mere hint as to the way in which she was to endeavor to gain an influence over Irma. He felt as sure of his wife's course in the matter as if she were a force in nature, and well knew that, if left to her own methods, the result would be so much the more certain.

Gunther usually kept his household free from all relations with the court; but this was the daughter of his friend--although that friend was angry at him--and he allowed her the freedom of his house.

Some weeks before, when speaking of the Te Deum on the occasion of the birth of the crown prince, Irma had casually referred to her having met

Gunther's wife and youngest daughter. The doctor had again, as if by the merest chance, introduced the subject, and, almost without knowing it, Irma had expressed a wish to improve the slight acquaintance thus begun. This was just what he wished for, and, on the afternoon of the day following, he conducted Irma to his beautiful, well-furnished home.

Gunther's wife was Swiss by birth, and had come from a wealthy and cultured family. She spoke High German with a strong Alemannic accent. She endeavored neither to retain the dialect nor to acquire the language of books. Her easy, natural ways seemed the result of careful culture, but there was no attempt to show off either. As a matter of course, she was perfectly conversant with all that related to the economy of the household, and at the same time fully alive to all that makes for beauty and the common weal.

As a singer, Madame Gunther had been a great favorite, both in social circles and at important vocal performances. Her voice was a full, resonant soprano and, although she had given up singing solos, she and her daughters would still take part when great musical works were performed. When fresher voices had taken the solo parts, she had, without a murmur of regret, retired to her place in the chorus.

And thus, too, was her life. Self-reliant and diligent at home, she took an active interest in all public institutions in which women were permitted to take part. She had preserved one priceless heirloom--she was free from nervousness and, with her, public spirit was a duty. She educated her children, managed her household, was a kind and attentive hostess, and performed all this as if obeying the simple instincts of her nature.

She honored her husband. Whatever he said was always of special weight, but still she held fast to her own judgment. Although she had been living in the capital for nearly twenty years, she had remained a stranger to the whole of the hodge-podge system of caste and the granting of favors by the grace of this or that one. She was not opposed to the system, but she left such matters to those in whose eyes they possessed value and importance; as for herself, she regarded them with absolute indifference.

She was pleased at the honors shown her husband, but that seemed, to her, a matter of course. He was a great man, and if the world had withheld its praise, he would, in her eyes, still have been the greatest and best of men. Her whole bearing expressed this feeling. She had never had the slightest desire to appear at court, and when her husband was obliged to be away from home by day or at night, and often for weeks at a time, she accepted his absence as unavoidably incident to his calling, and refrained from adding to his discomfort by complaining thereat.

When the doctor returned, it was always to a well-ordered home. Refreshed and invigorated by its influence, he would go back to the smooth and slippery precincts of the court.

Irma was now introduced to this home. In appearance, she was all beauty and dignity, and no one would have guessed how forlorn and homeless she felt within her heart. In her hand, she held the bouquet which had, as usual, been sent to her that day, by the king's orders. Gunther had told her that this was his daughter Paula's birthday, and she had brought the flowers for her. They were as lovely as she who brought them. And yet what was it that clung to them? It was almost sinful to use the bouquet as a birthday favor, for Irma felt mortified when she received it. But the flowers were as coin that might be passed on to another.

When Irma entered the house, she felt as if escaping from the noise and bustle of the market-place, or the restless life and cries of the highway, into a temple of domestic peace.

The house was on a little, narrow street, and was surrounded by a garden full of tall, fine trees. A portion of the yard had been fenced off and converted into an aviary. The hallway and rooms were adorned with statuettes and pictures; the furniture was simple and massive. The doctor's library, reception-room and study were in the upper story.

There had been no preparations of any kind for Irma's reception. The mother had carefully enjoined her daughters not to make any change in their dress on account of the countess's visit. They did not go out to meet her. She was conducted through the summer house, where the flowers and presents for Paula had been arranged, and there, on the steps, sat Madame Gunther and her daughters, busily engaged in needlework. The elder daughter, the wife of Professor Korn of the university, had her child with her. Paula, the younger of the two, who, like Irma, had just entered her twenty-first year, could not be termed beautiful, but had a bright and cheerful countenance and a fine figure.

Irma was warmly welcomed. As it was Gunther's hour for consultation, he soon retired and left her with the ladies. She was surprised, at first, to find herself repeatedly accosted as the daughter of an old friend. She was not here on her own merit, or as the most admired of all the ladies at court, but simply as Count Eberhard's daughter, who had been received into the house from an affectionate sense of duty. When asked about her father's health, she thanked them, although she felt sad at heart to think that she knew so little of him. How utterly different from hers was the life these children led.

Music soon afforded a convenient and agreeable change. On the piano, there lay a composition in manuscript. It was by a nephew of Madame Gunther's, who lived in northern Germany. Madame Gunther told her that he was a philologist by profession, but that, as he would, in all likelihood, lose his eyesight, he had determined to cultivate his decided musical gifts and to perfect himself as a musician.

Irma begged Madame Gunther to sing the song, but she replied that, while her voice was no longer equal to it, that of the countess was exactly suited to it. She gave the manuscript to Irma, who read it over and afterward sang it with rich, full voice, to Madame Gunther's accompaniment. The composition was pleasing, but full of suggestions of well-known masters.

Madame Gunther now showed what she meant by practical singing. Irma did not make the best use of the means at her command, and where there were faults showed them too plainly. The doctor's wife instructed her in a simple, unpretentious manner, and Irma remarked that the daughters ought to feel happy to think that they could hear such singing every day.

"And this is my son, the most grateful of all listeners," said Madame Gunther, introducing a handsome young man with a full, brown beard. He was technical director in a manufactory of chemicals, and had brought a student with him. Female friends who lived in the neighborhood joined them soon afterward, and there were merry times on the terrace and in the garden.

Irma remarked the attentive glances directed upon her. It seemed to her as if all knew the troubles that filled her soul; she had completely forgotten how beautiful she was.

"Pardon me, Madame Gunther, for looking at you so," said Irma, suddenly, "but I am somewhat of a dabbler in plastic art, and when I notice the contour and color of your head, it seems as if the Holbein Madonna, of the Dresden Gallery, had come to life and was standing before me."

"Can you really see the resemblance, at this late day?" asked Madame Gunther, blushing slightly; "in former days, it was often remarked and was almost the very first thing my husband said to me in Zurich, now well-nigh twenty-six years ago. On my mother's side I can trace my descent from the family of Burgomaster Maier, by whose orders the picture was originally painted."

Irma was delighted with all that she heard and saw, and especially with Madame Gunther's reminiscences. While speaking of her own efforts in the way of art, she looked at the doctor's wife earnestly, and only wished she were able to model a portrait, in which case Madame Gunther would have to sit to her. She could not help thinking, at the same time, that there was a culture which had been handed down from earliest times: a culture whose history, running through all ages, is entirely different from that of the nobility, and that the best results of human effort had been brought about, not by the nobles, but by civic liberty.

Madame Gunther asked Irma whether she had a picture of her mother.

Irma replied that her father had had a portrait taken of her mother when in the fullness of her beauty. The picture had been a failure, and almost seemed as if intended for some one else, and so her father had ordered it to be destroyed. He would rather have no picture than a false one.

"That, of itself, is enough to make one honor him for his love of truth," said Madame Gunther. "Most people are satisfied with what is false, and keep on saying: 'you can recognize this or that feature,' until they, at last, persuade themselves that it must once have been a true likeness."

The conversation now turned upon the fact that Irma had never known her mother, and Irma's glance often dwelt upon the two daughters sitting beside their mother.

Madame Gunther said:

"I trust that I've not awakened painful memories, but I regard it as a duty that we should often think of our beloved dead; calmly and peacefully, of course. I've always felt thus with regard to my departed mother, and I hope that, when the time comes, my children may have the same feelings toward me."

Irma pressed Madame Gunther's hand. All that she said was so full of truth, so satisfying.

Madame Gunther told her that it was long before she had acquired a taste for plastic art. Appreciation had, however, gradually dawned upon her; but it was for what related to the human figure, rather than for landscapes. The conversation continued in an easy and cheerful vein. The carriage had long ago been announced; the half-hour which Irma had meant to stay with Madame Gunther had been prolonged to more than an hour. At last, she took her leave with sincere requests to repeat her visit.

CHAPTER VIII

When Irma returned to the palace, she felt as if coming from another world--from a life far removed from her own.

Gunther was a deep student of the human heart.

In one respect, Irma's visit had had the result foreseen by him; but there was some unknown influence at work, and, perhaps, affecting previously existing conditions. Nothing unless it be the drop that falls from the cloud, is free from foreign admixture, and it is from pure thought alone that one can draw definite conclusions. The water in the spring, and the living human heart, both contain foreign elements within themselves, and no one can foretell how a new ingredient may affect the invisible atoms thus held in solution.

Irma's soul was deeply agitated. Her great power had been exercised and had sought some act in which to spend itself. She had felt happy in the possession of the king's friendship and in the thought that she could furnish so great a mind as his with the congenial companionship he would otherwise be obliged to forego; but the daily bouquet, trivial attention as it was, had aroused and offended her. "He isn't my ideal," said she to herself, and her heart felt lonely again, as it had been ever since she was old enough to think.

Although she had been lonely while at the cloister, she had there found a friend who, if she had little to impart, gratefully accepted all that Irma could give her. At the court, she felt lonely in spite of her wanton humors. She was always obliged to be doing something, be it playing, singing, painting or modeling; anything but this deathlike solitude. She was suffering the homesickness of the soul.

"Are not all in this world homeless?" she asked herself, and, while searching her mind for an answer, Gunther had introduced her to his household.

There, all seemed beautiful and complete. There was a home, and a mother who showed that she understood a young and ardent life; the daughters would never suffer as she did. The mother's glance fell upon her and seemed to say: "I shall understand you and will soothe all sorrows you may tell me of." But Irma could not complain, nor exclaim: "Help me!"--and where nothing was required of her, least of all. She could and must help herself.

Madame Gunther had touched her most tender chord: the memory of her mother, and, although Irma gently avoided the subject, her pain was so much the greater.

She wept, but did not know it until a tear dropped on her bosom.

There is so much comfort, so much of real and beautiful seclusion, in a world which is content with itself, and which, in its work and education, requires no favors from those above. How happy the lot of a daughter in such a home, until she, in turn, becomes the head of another household.

Irma felt humbled. All her pride had left her. Her thoughts were still in the garden, where the people moved about in careless unconstraint and where the men, returning from their professional labors, and the maidens, from their domestic duties, were enjoying themselves in common.

"One thing yet remains mine and it is the best," exclaimed Irma, suddenly rising: "solitude is mine. I can yet be lonely, strong, self-contained."

Her waiting-maid entered and announced a lackey sent by the queen.

"Does the queen want to see me at once?"

"Yes, gracious Countess."

"Very well, I'll be there directly."

"Walpurga was right, after all," said she to herself; "I, too, serve."

She felt vexed while she stood before the mirror to have her dress adjusted. She assumed a cheerful expression with which to appear before the queen. She was obliged to do so.

She hastened to obey the queen's orders. When she got near the door, she drew herself up and again fixed her features in the cheerful, smiling expression that she wished them to have, and then entered the room, which, as usual, was dimly lighted.

The queen was sitting in a large arm-chair. She was clad in a dress of snowy white, and a lace handkerchief had been twined about her golden hair.

"Come nearer, dear Countess," said the queen. "I am delighted to see you again. When I see my dear friends, it seems as if I'd been spending the last few weeks in another world. Unfortunately, I am somewhat indisposed again. I owe you special thanks, for I understand that you've kindly interested yourself in the nurse; by keeping her cheerful, you do the prince a service. The king quite agrees with me that you're a real treasure to us. I shall write as much to your father and tell him how happy we are to have you with us. That will surely put him in a better humor with you."

Irma was glad that the queen had so much to say, for she was thus enabled to recover her composure.

"Pray give me the letter that lies on the table," said the queen.

Irma brought it and the queen added:

"Just read these lines of the king's."

Irma read: "Pray tell Countess Irma to keep me constantly informed as to the condition of our son. Remember me to the dear fourth petal of our clover-leaf."

Irma returned the letter with thanks. She felt deeply humiliated to think that the king was trying to force her to write, and at the method he had chosen. Walpurga was right when she spoke of love-glances at the cradle.

Irma almost fainted with grief and shame.

"Won't you do us the favor to write, dear Countess?"

Irma bowed deeply, and the queen continued:

"Of course there will be very little to write about. Man is the highest object in creation and, for that very reason, develops far more slowly than all other creatures."

Irma was about to suggest that, at that rate, a prince would develop still more slowly, but she merely nodded and smiled assent.

She was not in a mood to enter into the queen's way of thinking. She could see nothing in her but nursery thoughts, with which, at present, she had no sympathy. Though they were vastly more important, what would it matter to me, thought she to herself. Here, just as in Gunther's house, there is a life separate from the world and contented with itself. Here is a mother and her child. Of what use am I? Merely to talk and take part in everything. All others are complete and possess a world of their own; and am I always only to take a part--there, the alms bestowed by friendship; here, those accorded me by royal grace? Am I complete in myself, or am I not?

And while Irma's mind was filled with these thoughts, the queen, in her agitated, soulful manner, went on to say:

"The miracle of life fills me with awe. Have you never thought of the world of meaning suggested by the idea of a child drawing its first breath and opening its eyes for the first time? Air and light are earth's first and last messengers; the first breath and the last; the first glance and the last. How wonderful!"

Irma now felt what it was to serve. Had she been free, and on an equal footing with the one who addressed her, she would have said: "My dear friend, I am not in the mood, just now, to enter into what you are saying. Within your soul, there is the calm of early morn; in mine, hot, burning noonday. I implore you, leave me to myself."

Irma was filled with a deep longing for boundless solitude, but she dared not show it. She would gladly have closed her eyes, but obsequious glances were required of her. She listened and answered, but her soul was far away. For the first time in her life, she felt indignant that there was a fellow-being who enjoyed rights of which she was deprived. She felt angry at the queen. She was, several times, on the point of mentioning her visit to Gunther's house, but felt that life there had nothing in common with the constant gloom of the queen's apartment. It seemed to her, moreover, that it were wrong, even in thought, to bring hither the citizen-wife whose footsteps had never entered the palace; and then she thought of her father and his strong sense of independence.

And while such were her thoughts, she spoke of the prince and of Walpurga's amusing peculiarities.

The queen saw that Irma's thoughts were slightly tinged with sadness and, wishing to cheer her up, said:

"Ah, dear countess, I am really languishing for music. Friend Gunther has forbidden my listening to music, lest it might affect my nerves; but one of your little songs would do no harm. I hear that you've learned a beautiful one from the nurse. Won't you sing it for me? May I send for your zither?"

Irma felt more like crying, but she bowed assent and sent a servant for the zither. He brought it, and Irma sang:

"Ah, blissful is the tender tie
That binds me, love, to thee,
And swiftly speed the hours by

When thou art near to me.

"My heart doth bear a burden, love,
And thou hast placed it there;
And I would wager e'en my life
That none doth heavier bear."

Within Irma's soul there was a shrill, discordant accompaniment to this song, every word of which had a double meaning.

"And I must sing this to the queen," said the voice within her. "Yes, you two are united. All happy ones are. The unhappy one is always lonely."

Her song was full of gloomy despair; her heart, of anger. "You sing that with deep feeling," said the queen, "and my son hears it, too. One can scarcely say 'hears,' for all that he hears or sees is undefined. Pray repeat the song, so that I may sing it to myself."

Irma sang it again, but this time her mind was more at ease. The queen thanked her heartily. "The doctor has unfortunately forbidden my conversing for any length of time, even with those who are dear to me. I am delighted to think that we shall soon go to the summer palace. Then we will spend much of our time together and with the child. Adieu! dear Countess, write soon, and sing your lovely soul into the child's heart."

Irma went away. While passing through the long corridors, she stopped several times, as if to remember where she was. At last she reached her room, and gave orders that her horse be saddled at once and that a groom be in waiting.

Irma had just changed her dress when a servant brought her a letter. She broke the seal with a trembling hand and read:

"*My child*: You have now been at court for eighteen months. I have left you free and uncontrolled. There are many things which I would like to say to you, but cannot write. Writing estranges. Your rooms are ready, and flowers await you. It is now lovely summer and apples on your tree are getting ruddy cheeks like your own, and I should like to see yours again. Come to

"Your Father."

Irma threw up her hands. "This is deliverance! Yes, I still have a home, and there is still a heart against which I can rest my head. I am coming, father! I am coming!"

Her brain whirled with excitement. She rang for her servant and sent word to the groom that she would not ride out. Then, after having ordered the waiting-maid to pack up enough clothes for several weeks, as quickly as possible she presented herself before the queen and asked for leave of absence.

"I am sorry that you, too, leave me," said the queen, "but I shall gladly part with you if it only helps, as I hope it will, to make you happy. Do all that lies in your power to be in full accord with your father. Believe me, Irma, in the various relations of life, be it as wife or as mother, one is sensible of a constant desire to grow and expand with each succeeding day; the child alone is perfectly satisfied with itself."

The queen and Irma were not in accord that day. Irma was restless and anxious to depart. Whatever detained her, though it were only for a second, excited her resentment.

What the queen was saying might have been interesting to one who was not in a hurry, but not to her whose foot was already on the carriage step.

The parting was, nevertheless, an affecting one, the queen kissing Irma.

All that now remained was to ask Countess Brinkenstein's formal assent That, too, was obtained.

She had not yet said farewell to Doctor Gunther and his family. She wished to say good-by through Colonel Bronnen, or Baron Schoning, who had told her that he often visited the doctor's house. It was also necessary to take leave of these men and her companions at court. Now that she was about to go, she found out how many acquaintances she had. But where are they when you need them? They are here, simply that you may not need them. Such is the world; but stop! There's one to whom, of all others, you must say farewell. She hurried off to Walpurga.

"Walpurga," she exclaimed, "when you get up tomorrow, shout as loud as you can. By that time, I'll be at our mountain home, and I'll shout back to you until the whole world rings with laughter. I'm going to my father."

"I'm glad of it."

"And aren't you sorry to see me go?"

"Of course; but if your father's still alive you oughtn't miss looking into the eyes that are only once in the world for you. I'm glad, for your father's sake, that he's able to look on such a child as you are. Oh! if my Burgei were only as tall."

"Walpurga, I'll also go to see your husband, your child and your mother. I'll sit down at your table and remember you to your cow and your dog. I shall; depend upon it."

"Oh! how happy they'll be! If Hansei's only at home and not in the woods."

"If he is, I'll have them send for him; and now farewell! don't forget me!"

"You can rely on that," said Walpurga, while Irma hurried away.

She still found time to write to her friend Emma:

"*Dearest Emma*: Two hours ago, I received a letter from father. He calls me home to him. I have leave of absence for a fortnight. Do you know what that means? I was obliged to promise that I would surely return; I don't know whether I shall keep my promise. The earth trembles at my feet and my head swims. The world is all chaos, but there will be light! Any one can say: 'Let there be light!' If we only could always do our best. But I shall not write another word. It is enough; I shall see you soon. Come to Wildenort as soon as you can, to your

"Irma.

"P.S.--I shall take no excuse; you must come. In return, I promise to go to your wedding. Many greetings to all of yours, and, above all, to your Albrecht."

The sun was already sinking toward the horizon, when Irma, accompanied by her maid, departed for Wildenort.

CHAPTER IX

So one can go away, after all, and leave the motley monotony called "the world" behind. Farewell, thou palace, and furnish thy inmates with their daily pleasures. Farewell, ye streets, filled with shops and offices, towers and churches, theaters, music halls and barracks. May fashion be gracious and favor you with customers, clients, guests, applause, and fostering laws. Vanish, frail frippery! I feel like a bird flying from the housetop, out into the wide world. How foolish to remain in the cage when the door is always open. Thou, great bailiff who holds the world captive--thy name is custom!

Thus thought Irma to herself, while seated in the carriage and driving out into the open world.

Her thoughts again recurred to the great house which she had just left. It was the dinner hour and they were waiting for the queen to appear. What a pity that the lord steward had not been present at the creation of the world, for here every one has his fixed place and the service is simply perfect. The queen expresses her regrets at the departure of Countess Irma. All praise her.

"Oh, she's so very good," says one.

"And so merry," says another.

"Somewhat unmanageable, but very amiable," says still another.

But what is there new? It's a bore to be talking of one subject all the time. Help! Zamiel Schnabelsdorf!

"Away with it all!" exclaimed Irma, suddenly: "I shall not look back again, but forward to my father."

The horses stepped out bravely, as if they knew they were carrying a child to her father.

Irma was so impatient that she told the servant who was seated on the box, to give a double fee to the driver so that they might get on faster.

She could hardly wait until she saw her father, so anxious was she to rest her head upon his breast.

What did she desire? To complain to him? How could he help her? She knew not. All she knew was that, with him, there must be peace. She wished to be sheltered, protected; no longer alone. To obey him and anticipate his every wish would be her highest happiness. To be released from herself, and to desire nothing that did not minister to the joy of another--oh, how happy the thought! The whole earthly load is removed. Thus must it be with the blessed spirits above! Thus should we imagine angels to be! They want for nothing and need nothing, they never change and never grow, are neither young nor old. They are eternal, and are ever laboring for and through others. Their works bring joy to the world and to themselves. They are the undying rays of an eternal sun.

During the greater part of the journey, Irma's brain was filled with such unintelligible dreams, and the whole world seemed to be saying: "Father--Daughter."

She regained composure at last. It would not do to arrive at the castle in this state.

Agitation is weakness, and it had always been her father's aim to foster strength of mind and self-command.

Irma forced herself to observe what was going on about her.

It was twilight when they reached the first post-station. Irma fancied she could almost feel the air of her native mountains, although they were still far off.

They drove on at a rapid pace. The evening bells were ringing, and the air was filled with their sounds, carrying them out to the men and women in the fields, and measuring time and eternity for them.

What would the world be without its bells, whose pealing harmonies are to serve as a substitute for the beautiful creations of antique art?

But these thoughts failed to satisfy Irma. They lifted her out of the world, whilst she desired to occupy herself with what was present and established.

In the villages through which they drove, and the fields by which they passed, there was singing, interrupted, now and then, by the rattling of the carriage wheels, and Irma thought: We make too much noise in this world, and thus miss enjoying what the rest may have to tell us.

No thoughts were to her liking. No outlook pleased her.

The stars appeared in the heavens, but what were they to man? They shine for him who is free and has naught to seek on earth. She, however, was seeking, and, in the world's vast circle, could see nothing but two starry eyes directed upon her; and they were her father's.

They continued on their journey, disturbing lazy horses and sleepy postilions at every station.

It was long after midnight when they arrived at Wildenort.

Irma alighted at the manor-house and, accompanied by the servant, knocked at the door.

Her father had not expected her so soon. There were no lights in the large house, or its extensive outbuildings.

Dogs barked, for strangers were coming. There was not even a dumb beast that knew Irma, for she was a stranger in her father's house.

Two plowboys passed by. They were astonished to see the beautiful lady at that hour, and she was obliged to tell them who she was.

She ordered her rooms to be opened. Her father slept near by. She longed to see him, but controlled herself. He could sleep calmly and not know that she was breathing near him. She, too, soon fell asleep and did not wake till broad daylight.

Stepping softly, old Eberhard entered the ante-chamber where Irma's maid was already sitting.

"My lady the countess, is still sleeping. It was three o'clock, just about daybreak, when we arrived."

"What made you hurry so and take no rest?"

"I don't know; but the countess was quite excited on the way. They couldn't drive fast enough for her. When my lady wishes anything, it must be done at once."

"Who are you, dear child?"

"Her ladyship's maid."

"No, but who are your parents? What took you to court?"

"My father was riding-master to Prince Adolar, and her royal highness had me educated in the convent school."

A chain of dependents, from generation to generation, thought the old man to himself.

The maid looked at him wonderingly.

He was tall and broad-shouldered.

He wore the mountaineer's dress and a white horn whistle hung by a cord from his neck. His fine head bent slightly forward and rested on a massive neck; his gray hair and beard were thick and closely cropped; his brown eye still sparkled, as if in youth; his expressive countenance looked like embossed work, and his whole figure resembled that of a knight who has just laid aside his armor and put himself at ease.

"I wish to see my daughter," said the old man as he went into the adjoining room. It was dark. Eberhard stepped to the window, on tiptoe and drew aside the green damask curtain. A broad ray of light streamed into the room. He stood before the bed and, with bated breath, watched the sleeping one.

Irma was beautiful to behold. Her head, encircled by the long, loosened, golden-brown tresses; the clear, arched brow, the delicately chiseled nose, the mouth with its exquisitely curved upper lip, the rosy chin, the full cheeks with their peach-like glow--over all there lay a calm and peaceful expression. The beautiful, small, white hands lay folded on her breast.

Irma was breathing heavily, and her lips moved as if with a sad smile. It is difficult to sleep with one's hands folded on the breast. The hands gently loosened themselves, but the left one still rested on her heart. The father lifted it carefully and laid it at her side. Irma slept on quietly. Silently, the father took a chair and sat down at her bedside. While he sat there, two doves alighted on the broad window-sill, where they remained cooing with each other. He would have liked to frighten them away, but he dared not stir. Irma slept on and heard nothing.

Suddenly the pigeons flew away, and Irma opened her eyes.

"Father!" she cried, throwing her arms around his neck and kissing him. "Home again! Oh, how happy it makes me! Do draw the other curtain, so that I can see you better, and pray open the window so that I may inhale my native air! Oh, father! I've been away and now I've come back to you, and you won't let me go away again. You will support me in your powerful arms. Oh, now I think of what you said to me in my dream. We were standing together up on the Chamois hill and you took me up in your arms and, while carrying me, said: 'See, my child; so long as one of your parents lives, there is some one to help you bear up in the world.' Oh, father! Where have I been? Where am I now?"

"Be calm, my child. You've been at court and now you're home again. You're excited. Calm yourself. I'll call the servant. Breakfast is ready in the arbor."

He kissed her forehead and said:

"I kiss all your good and pure thoughts, and now let us live together again, as plain and sensible beings."

"Oh, that voice! To be in my father's house and at home once more. Life elsewhere is just like sleeping in one's clothes. 'Tis only at home that one can rest; for there no bond oppresses us."

He was about to leave, but Irma detained him.

"I feel so happy," said she, "to be here and look at you; to see you and think of you, all the time."

The father passed his hand over her forehead, and she said:

"Let your hand rest there. I now believe in the laying on of hands; my own experience convinces me."

He remained at her bedside for some time, his hand still resting upon her forehead.

At last he said:

"And now arise, my child. I shall expect you at breakfast."

"I am glad there is some one who can command me to 'get up.'"

"I don't command, I simply advise you. But, my dear child, something strange must be going on with you, as you understand nothing in its literal sense."

"Yes, father,--very strange! but that's all over, now."

"Well then, follow me as soon as you can; I shall await you."

The father went out to the arbor, where he awaited her coming. He moved the two cups and the beautiful vase of flowers first to one position, and then to another, and arranged the white table-cloth. Shortly after, Irma entered, clad in a white morning dress.

"You're--you're taller than I thought you were," said the father, a bright color suffusing his face.

He stroked his daughter's cheek, while he said:

"This white spot on your rosy cheek, extending from the jaw to the cheek-bone, is just as your mother had it."

Irma smiled and, grasping both of her father's hands, looked into his eyes. Her glance was so full of happiness that the old man, who, at all times, preserved his equanimity, found his eyes filling with tears. He endeavored to conceal them, but Irma said:

"That won't in the least detract from your heroism. Oh, father, why are we such slaves to ourselves? Why should we be afraid to appear as we are? Your great rule is that we should follow out our natures. Why do we not always do so? Oh, father, let me send up a joyful shout to my native mountains, to the forests and the lakes! I'm with ye, again, my constant friends! Let us live together! Hold fast by me and I will be as faithful as ye are! I greet thee, sun; and yonder hill under which my mother rests--"

She could not go on. After some time, the old man said:

"It would be well, my child, if we could live out our life in all its native purity; but it is neither fear of ourselves, nor self-imposed slavery that induces us to avoid such scenes, such violent agitation. It is a deep-seated feeling that, by contrast, the next moment must appear bald and commonplace. It would oblige us to plunge from a life of excessive sensibility into the every-day world. It is for this reason that we should, and do, exercise self-control; for such emotions should not exhaust themselves in what might be called a devout outburst, but should extend through all our acts and thoughts, even to the smallest and most insignificant. That is the source of our noblest aspiration. Yes, my child, the very ones who thus, as it were, divide their life in two, profane the one-half of it, while they secretly flatter themselves: We have had great and noble emotions and are still capable of feeling them."

The old housekeeper brought the coffee. Irma waited on her father and told him that she expected Emma and her betrothed. Eberhard said:

"When Emma was here, years ago, your thoughts ran in the same vein as at present. We were on the Chamois hill, where a fine view of the great lake can be obtained, and were waiting to see the sunrise. Emma, in her matter-of-fact and plain-spoken way, said: 'I don't think it worth while to lose one's sleep and go to so much trouble for this. I find the sunset fully as beautiful and far less troublesome.' What did you answer her at the time?"

"I can't remember, father, dear."

"But I do. You said: 'The sunrise is far more elevating, but I don't know what one can do to have the rest of the day in keeping with the lofty mood thus inspired. Sunset is better for us, because the world then veils itself and allows us to rest. After beholding the highest, there are only two things left us--sleep and music.'"

"But, father, I've ceased to think so. Yesterday, during the whole of my drive, I was haunted by the thought: What are we in the world for, after all? Without us the trees would still grow; the beasts, the birds and the fishes would still live without us. All these have a purpose in the world; man alone is obliged to seek one. Men paint, and build, and till the soil, and study how they may the better kill each other. The only difference, after all, between mankind and the beast is that man buries his dead."

"And have you ventured so far, my child? I am indeed glad that you're with me once again. You must have had much to contend with. I trust you will once more learn to believe that our proper destiny is, to live in accordance with nature and reason. Look at the world!" said he, with a smile. "A maiden twenty-one years of age, and a countess to boot, asks: 'Why am I in the world?' Ah, my child, to be beautiful, to be good, to be as lovely as possible in mind as well as in outward form. Conduct yourself so that you can afford to wish that every one might know you thoroughly.--But enough of this, for the present."

The hour that father and daughter thus spent together in the arbor was full of happiness for both, and Irma repeatedly expressed a wish that she could thus live forever.

Oblivious of all else, each seemed to constitute the other's world.

"You've become my great tall girl," said her father. He had intended to say: "You must have gone through a great deal, for you return to your father and have nothing to tell about matters trifling or personal to yourself." He had intended to say this, but simply repeated: "You've become my great girl."

"And, father! you order me to remain with you, do you not?"

"You know very well that I've never ordered you to do anything, since you were able to think for yourself," replied the father. "I'd have you act according to your own convictions, and not against your will or reason."

Irma was silent. She had not received the answer she had hoped for, and, feeling that she must herself bring about the desired result, determined to do so.

A forest-keeper came to receive instructions in regard to the woods. Eberhard replied that he would ride out there himself. Irma begged to be allowed to accompany him and, her father consenting, she soon appeared in a hunting-dress and rode off with him across the meadows and in the direction of the forest.

Her face glowed with animation while she felt herself moving along on the spirited steed, through the shady, dewy forest.

While her father was giving his orders to the forest-keepers, Irma was resting on a mossy bank under a broad spreading fir tree. Her father's dog had already made friends with her, and now came up and licked her hand. Thus awakened, she arose and walked over toward the field at the edge of the forest. The first object her eyes fell upon was a four-petaled clover-leaf. She quickly possessed herself of it. Her father now joined her and noticed her happy looks.

"How much good it has done me to rest on the earth," said she.

He made no reply. He did not think it necessary that every feeling, however deep, should find vent in words.

Irma looked up in surprise. In the world of conversation, small change is paid back for every remark.

They soon returned home.

During the afternoon they were seated together in the cool library. Cicero's words, "When I am alone, then am I least alone," were written in letters of gold, over the door.

The father was writing and would occasionally look at his daughter, who was engaged with a volume of Shakespeare. She was reading the noblest thoughts, taking them up into herself, and making them a part of her own soul.

Eberhard felt it a joy to detect his own glance in another's eye, to hear his own thoughts from other lips, and that eye and those lips his child's--to note that her soul reflected his, although native temperament and peculiar impressions had served to make hers different from and independent of his own. The ideal that had filled his youthful dreams now stood before him, incarnate.

Eberhard soon closed his book and smiled to himself. He was not so strong as he had imagined. Now that his child was with him, he could not keep on with his work, as he had done the day before. He sat down by Irma, and, pointing to Spinoza's and Shakespeare's works, that always lay on his work-table, he said:

"To them, the whole world was revealed. Although they lived centuries ago, they are my constant companions on these lonely mountains. I shall pass away and leave no trace of my thoughts behind me, but I've already lived the life eternal in the companionship of the noblest minds. The tree and the beast live only for themselves, and during the short period that ends with death. With life, we inherit the result of centuries of thought and he who, within himself, has become a true man fully embodies the idea of humanity. Thus you live on, with your father and with all that is true and beautiful in the history of the human race."

There was a long pause. It was, at last, broken by the father's saying:

"Didn't you come in a court carriage?"

"Certainly."

"And so you intend to return to court?"

"Father, don't let us speak of that, now. I've not, like you, strength enough to drop from the greatest heights down to the level of every-day life."

"My child, every-day affairs are the highest that can engage us."

"But I'd like to forget that there is such a thing as a court, or that I've ever been, or ever shall be, anything but part of your heart and soul."

"No, you're to live for yourself; but if you wish to remain with me, all you need do is to send the carriage back."

"I shall have to return, though it be but for a few days. I have only leave of absence, not a discharge. The best thing would be for you to go with me and bring me back again."

"I can't go to court, as you well know; and I give you credit for enough strength to take yourself away from there. I was watching you to-day while you lay asleep. There's nothing false in you; as yet, no evil passions cloud your brow. I know your brother is anxious to have you marry, and I, too, wish that you may become a good wife and mother. But I fear that you have become too much your own, ever to become another's. Be that as it may, my child, look at the scene spread out before you. Myriads of flowers are blooming silent and unknown. Should a wanderer pass by and feast his eyes upon them, or even pluck a flower, it has lived for him. Should it blossom and fade away unseen, it has lived for itself. But, my child, don't go out of your way to please me. How long is your leave?"

"A fortnight."

"Let us spend the time in truth and cheerfulness, and then act as your judgment dictates."

CHAPTER X

The days passed by quickly. Eberhard had little to do with his neighbors, but was always glad to see the burgomaster of the village, who was, also, a deputy to the Diet, and to consult with him regarding the affairs of the community.

Irma spent much of her time alone. She read, embroidered, painted and sang. After the first few days, a reaction set in.

"What is this life?" she asked herself, "of what use? I work for dress--dress for my soul and for my body. And to what purpose? The mirror sees me, the walls hear me, and I have my father for one hour at noon and another in the evening."

She endeavored to control her flights, and, although she succeeded in that, could not prevent herself from thinking of one who was distant. She would look around as if she could hear his footsteps and as if the air were filled with his presence; and that man was--the king.

She could not but think that he expected a letter from her, and what had he received? The news of her departure. Why should she insult and mortify him?

While at Wildenort, she was several times on the point of writing to him. She wanted to tell him that she had meant to flee from him; nay, from herself. Framing the sentences in her mind, she would say to herself: Flight is not cowardice. Indeed, it requires great strength thus to tear one's self away. She meant to make this clear to him. She did not wish him to think ill of humanity and, least of all, of her. His great and extended energy should not be weakened, or even disturbed, by the consciousness that mankind had no conception of the truly noble. She owed it, both to him and to herself, to explain this; but it is difficult to do it all in writing. She would, therefore, return and tell him all, and, after that, they would, although distant, be united in the noblest thoughts. She felt satisfied that she would find full compensation for a lonely life in the recollection of one moment of perfect communion with a noble mind, and the consciousness of truth and purity in thought and deed.

Irma was delighted to think that she had thus liberated herself.

She refrained, as far as possible, from speaking to her father about the court; but a remark would, now and then, involuntarily escape her, and she would tell how the king and the queen had praised this or that, or had uttered such and such a remark, and it was easily to be seen that she attached special importance to what they had said.

"That's the way with men," said Eberhard, smiling. "They know what they are, or, at least, ought to; and yet they give a prince the right to stamp them with a value. It is he who determines: you are worth so and so much; you a ducat, you a thaler, you a mere brass counter, you a privy councilor and you a colonel. The story of the creation of the world is thus ever renewed. There it says that the Creator led the beasts out before man so that he might give them names. Here the human animals come to the prince and say; 'Give us a name, or we shall feel as if naked and be afraid.'"

Irma started at these harsh words. Solitude had brought her father to this point. She could not refrain from saying:

"You do the king great injustice; he has a noble mind and is full of intelligence."

"Intelligence! I know all about that," replied Eberhard. "He can ask questions without number, propound problems and, for his dessert, would fain have an epitome of ecclesiastical history, physiology or any other interesting department of knowledge. But he never applies himself; never reads a work through. He requires excerpts and essences. I know all about it. And the courtly roulade singers place their thoughts at his service. Don't imagine, my child, that I underrate the king's efforts. They've always told him: 'You are a genius!' They are always persuading kings that they possess genius, either military, political or artistic. All who approach a monarch are obliged, even in an intellectual sense, to attire themselves in court dress. He never sees men and things in their true colors; they all drape themselves to please him. Nevertheless, I believe the king honestly endeavors to see things as they are, and that's a great deal; but he can't shake off the magic spell of set forms and phrases."

Irma's lips trembled with emotion. She did not believe that her father meant to weaken her interest in the king, since he could not know of its existence; but his antagonism irritated her and she saw, with alarm, that no help was to be looked for in that quarter. She might have shared her father's solitude, if he had honored the exalted man as she did. He might have done homage to the noble mind, even though it was a monarch's, without doing violence to his republican feelings, or his sense of justice. But now he destroyed every bridge that had led to a better understanding and to justice. If another had spoken thus of the king, she would have made him feel her wrath, and now she felt that her silence was a sufficient sacrifice to filial duty. Her heart seemed to close up within itself, as if never again to be opened. She was a stranger in her father's house, and now doubly felt that she had never been at home there. She forced herself to appear cheerful and tranquil.

Eberhard observed that an inner conflict agitated her, and thought it was merely a struggle between court life and solitude. He did not aid her, for he thought that she could best gain peace if she fought the battle for herself.

On Sunday morning--Eberhard never went to church--he said:

"Have you time to listen to a long story?"

"Certainly."

"Then let me make my will while I am yet in health."

"Pray, father, don't do that. Spare me!"

"I don't mean as to my possessions, but as to myself. We have no picture of your dear mother, and none of you children have any idea of her appearance--so pure, so lovely, so full of sunshine; and, for that reason, I mean to give you a picture of my life. Treasure it. Who knows when I may again have a chance? If there's anything that you don't understand or that seems to you in danger of being misinterpreted, ask me about it. I don't find such objections an interruption. I pursue my life in its even tenor; nothing disturbs me. I've accustomed myself to improve my estate, to give orders to my servants and to answer their questions, and, afterward, to take up the train of thought just where it was broken off; and so you, too, may interrupt me whenever you care to.

"My father, who was a free count, was always proud of his direct relations to the empire. Unto his last day, he would never acknowledge the unity of the kingdom and would always ask; 'How goes it over there?' He regarded his domain as distinct from the rest, and his family as on an equality with all princely houses."

"And why, dear father," asked Irma, "would you destroy these beautiful memories that have been handed down from generation to generation?"

"Because history itself has destroyed them, and justly too. It is necessary for the preservation of mankind that new races should constantly ascend to the surface; but I didn't mean to tell you about my father. I spent a happy youth in this house. My preceptor, although an ecclesiastic, was a man of liberal opinions. I entered the military service a year before my father's death and, though I say it myself, presented no mean figure while there, for I possessed good looks and an iron frame. I was stationed with my regiment, in a fortress belonging to the confederation. While recklessly riding one day, I fell from my horse and dislocated my hip. It laid me up for a long time and thus afforded me an opportunity to become better acquainted with our regimental surgeon, Doctor Gunther. Has he never told you of the times we passed together?"

"He has merely mentioned them. It was only a few days ago that the king told me I was right in saying that Doctor Gunther would only furnish verbal prescriptions when they were demanded and were really necessary."

"Ah! and so the king said that you were right? 'You are right'--that is a real mark of grace and should make one happy for a whole day and perhaps even longer. Isn't it so?"

"Father--didn't you mean to tell me more about your life with Gunther?"

"Ah, my child, that was a wondrous time. As far as I was able, I dived, with him, into the study of philosophy. I can still remember, as if it were this very moment, the very hour and the very place by the fortress wall--it was a dull evening in autumn; I can still see the leaves as they fell from the trees--when Gunther for the first time, explained to me the great saying of the all-wise one: 'Self-preservation is the first law of nature.' I stood as if rooted to the spot; it dawned upon me like a revelation, and has never since left me. Although at times obscured by the events of life, 'preserve thyself,' has always been before my mind. I have faithfully lived up to the great precept, and alas, as I now see, too completely and selfishly. The man who lives only for himself does not live a complete life, but I can confess this to you, of all others, without fear. It was only later that I came thoroughly to know the great right of sovereignty that belongs to every human being. I had done much thinking before that, but never in logical connection. You cannot imagine what courage it requires, on the part of a favorite and respected officer, to venture on the study of philosophy; how opposed it is to the very idea of military service, how improper it seems to one's superiors, and how ridiculous to one's comrades. Military service so exhausts the body, by daily, and for the greater part, useless exercises, that it renders it difficult to cultivate one's mind. I often excused myself, as unwell, and remained in my room during the loveliest weather, simply on account of my studies. Our regiment was ordered to the capital, and Gunther accepted my offer of a discharge. He became a professor and I attended lectures. But I was painfully conscious of my deficiency in knowledge and ardently longed for a chance to devote my life to perfecting my education. An unforeseen event helped to bring about the desired end. I had become gentleman of the bedchamber and spent much of my time at court. At that early day, I observed the ineradicable, servile spirit that dwells in man. Every one rejoices that there are others lower down in the scale than himself, and is willing, on that account, to suffer some to stand above him. Princes are not to blame for this ladder of nonsense. One day while at the summer palace, the king had gone out hunting, and although it was long past the dinner hour, not a glimpse of him was to be seen. The chamberlains and the court ladies--I forget their titles--were walking in the park. They would sit down on the benches, look through their spy-glasses, and endeavor, unsuccessfully however, to keep up a sustained conversation; for the ladies and gentlemen, both young and old, were possessed of vulgar hunger. And still the herdsman who was to put fodder in the rack for them, did not make his appearance. Your uncle Willibald pacified his gnawing hunger with little biscuits, which did not destroy his appetite. Hours passed, while they walked about like Jews on the Day of Atonement. But they laughed and joked--at least they tried to--while their stomachs growled. And though your uncle had thirty horses in his stable at home, with oxen and cows and many broad acres besides, he was content to serve and wait there, because he took great pride in being lord chamberlain. At that time, my child, I was as old as you are now, and I swore to myself never more to be a servant to any man. At last, the king's hunting carriage arrived. All were profuse in their greetings and received him with smiling faces. And yet his majesty was in a bad humor, for while he had been unsuccessful, General Kont, who had been one of the hunting party, had committed the impropriety of shooting a deer with twelve antlers. The general felt very unhappy at his good luck, and his head hung as mournfully as that of the dead beast. He apologized again and expressed his regrets that his majesty had not killed the stag. With rueful countenance, the monarch congratulated him. The king looked at me and asked 'How are you?'

"'Very hungry. Your Majesty,' was my answer. The king smiled, but the rest of the court were horror-struck at my impertinence.

"We were obliged to wait another half-hour, while the king changed his dress and, at last, we went to dinner.

"My child, if you were to tell the story to a courtier, he would consider me intolerably stupid; but that meal was the last I ever ate at princely table.

"I know that I'm talkative--I'm an old man. I merely wanted to say: Look about you and see how many human sacrifices they are constantly requiring.

"The idea of princely dignity is a noble and beautiful one. The prince should embody the unity of the state; but, although the idea, in itself, is beautiful, the knowledge that its realization requires a pyramid of worn-out creatures, divested of human dignity, renders it repulsive to me.

"Irma, I feel as if I must impress the testament of my soul upon yours. The moment you feel that you've lost the smallest portion of your crown of human dignity, flee, without hatred or contempt; for he who carries such feelings in his soul is heavily laden and can never breathe freely. I don't hate the world; neither do I despise it. It simply appears to me strange, decayed, distant. Nor can I hate or despise any one, because his belief is different from mine.

"But as I don't wish to teach you, I will go on with my story. I applied for my discharge and entered the university as a student. I soon left, however, in order to continue my education in an agricultural school. After that, I traveled and, as you know, spent an entire year in America. I had a great desire to become acquainted with that new phase of history in which men are born to intellectual freedom and are not constantly looking back toward Palestine, Greece or Rome. I don't find the world of the future in America. All there is still, as it were, in a state of ferment suggestive of primeval processes; but whether a new civilization will be the result, is more than I know. I do know, however, that all mankind is patiently waiting for a new moral compact. But I, and many more of us, will never live to see it realized.

"Will the world of the future be governed by pure ideas, or will it again look up to some lofty personage as its exemplar? I should wish for the former, but its realization seems far off.

"Now to continue with the story of my life.

"I returned home and, meeting your mother, was unutterably happy. She was alone in the world. I have enjoyed the greatest of all happiness; there is none other like it. Three years after you were born, your mother died. I cannot give you particulars about her. Her whole appearance was one of strength and purity. The world regarded her as cold and reserved, but she was ardent and open-hearted, beautiful to her very heart, but only for me. I know that if she had been spared to me, I would have become one of the best and kindest of men. I dare not think of that.

"It was not to be.

"But I feel as if sanctified through her, for since that time no base thought has ever entered my soul; nor have I ever committed a deed that I should feel ashamed to confess to my daughter.

"She died, and I stood alone, my violent nature confronting the enigma of life.

"Although I could not give my children a stepmother, I became a stepfather to them. Yes, let me speak on: I am unsparing toward myself. I know that if others heard me, they would say that I am using too strong language. It is the fashion to be indulgent nowadays, but I am not in the mode. I put my children away from me. I placed you with your aunt, until you entered the convent, and Bruno remained with me until he went to the seminary. You were in fine institutions, with expensive fees, but you were nevertheless put away from me. You did not know your father; you merely knew that he was alive, but did not live with him. You grew up like orphaned children.

"It is only two years since I confessed this to myself. For weeks, it robbed me of sleep, of feeling and of thought, and still I adhered to it. The demon called sophistry was ever telling me: 'You could have been of no use to your children. You had still too much to do for yourself, and it is better for them that they should become free human agents through their own unaided efforts than through you.' There may be some truth in it, but nevertheless, I've put my children away from me."

The old man paused. Irma laid her hand upon his and gently stroked it.

"'Tis well. I've said it at last.

"I remained here, leading a solitary but not a lonely life. I communed with the greatest minds and, at the same time, easily managed our estate.

"I devoted myself to national affairs, but soon withdrew. I can't belong to a party, not even to the one that calls itself the party of freedom. It includes many noble-hearted men whom I honor and respect, but they put up with too many frivolous comrades who, while they prate of equality and of the highest good of man, do not hesitate to sacrifice their fellow-beings to themselves. Aristocratic triflers are simply vicious, but democratic triflers are corrupters of ideas. He who dare not wish that the whole people should think and act as he does, has no right to term himself a free and honest man.

"If liberty does not rest on morality, what is there to distinguish it from tyranny? What is tyranny? The egotistical abuse of beings endowed with equal rights to ourselves. A tyrant, in effect, denies his God. A frivolous democrat blasphemes Him. By the term God, I mean the full conception of the world's moral law. I was a hermit in the midst of the crowd, and am happier and more consistent, when away from the world.

"And now I am here leading a solitary life."

"Isn't it sad to be so lonely?" asked Irma.

"If I felt lonely, it would be very hard," replied Eberhard; "but man should not feel lonely, though he be alone. *Ennui* and loneliness have no resting-place here. Men who are nothing to themselves are lonely wherever they be; but let me continue my story.

"Gunther's defection caused me the greatest sorrow, but I was unjust toward him. He always was a friend of court life and regarded it as the culmination of culture. He was always too æsthetic and would often say: 'I, too, have a claim on the luxuries, the comforts, the pleasures of life and am determined to have my share of them.' That led him to court and caused him to desert free science and, at the same time, to lose both himself and me.

"You have probably been told, and have perhaps even yourself thought, that I am a misanthrope. He who hates mankind is a vain fool. In what respect is he better than the rest, or different from them? I don't hate mankind. I only know that most of them, either by their own efforts or through those of others, appear in false colors. They affect an interest in things that do not concern them and, in most instances, do not even know that it is affectation. I have often been deceived and cheated, but, I frankly confess, it was because I deceived myself. I gave forth what was best in me, and imagined that others were with me, but it was mere politeness that induced them to assent. They were not hypocrites; it was I who deceived myself. I imagined myself in a world in which all was peace and harmony, while, in fact, I was alone, completely alone. Every one who has a character of his own, is alone. There is no such thing as perfect accord; to live out one's self is all that remains. But most men do not care to do this, and they are best off. They live as custom and morals require, and do not greatly concern themselves about the present or the past. They jump or dawdle as the case may be from mood to mood, from enjoyment to enjoyment, and as long as they can always see the same face when they look in the glass, are perfectly content. Such faces never change. If the human countenance always expressed the thoughts that fill the soul, you would not be able to recognize any one from day to day, or even from hour to hour. I do not know, my child, where I am leading you to; I only meant to tell you that I am not a misanthrope. I love all men. I know that, at bottom, they cannot be different from what they are, and that honest nature still lies concealed beneath their frizzled, overloaded, glittering masks. They cannot reveal it, however, and in spite of their false, cunning ways, there still remains a great and wise precept: 'Forgive them, for they know not what they do.' And now let me add that I forgive your brother, too. He has deeply mortified me, for the deepest mortification that one can suffer is at the hands of one's child.

"I cannot force Bruno to act against his will, nor do I wish to. It is a strange world. The struggle between father and son drags on through all ages. My son defends the old, and I the new; but I must bear with it all.

"Freedom alone accords with the dictates of nature and reason. But you cannot force one to be free; nor do I wish to force you, in any way. Most women would rather yield to nature than affection, but I do not regard you as an ordinary woman, nor do I wish you to be one. You should--"

Although Eberhard had said that he did not wish to be interrupted, something now came which did interrupt him.

It was a messenger with a letter for Irma. She recognized the handwriting of her friend Emma, and hurriedly opening the letter, read as follows:

"*Irma*: I cannot come to thee. I have said farewell to the world. Three weeks ago to-day, my Albrecht lost his life through the bite of a mad dog. My life for this world is also at an end. I humbly submit to the inscrutable will of the Almighty. I have vowed to take the veil. I am here now, and shall never again leave this spot. Come, as soon as thou canst, to thy

"Sister Euphrosyne,

"In the convent of Frauenwörth."

Irma handed the letter to her father to read.

"And so the bite of a mad dog has destroyed two human lives. Who will explain this?" exclaimed Irma.

"In that respect, religion is just as impotent as we are. Like reason, she commands us to obey nature's law."

The messenger waited, and Irma went off to write an answer in which she promised to come.

Meanwhile, Eberhard sat alone. He had confided the story of his life to his child--and what would it avail? How often had he realized that no teaching, be it ever so noble, can change the human mind. Life, observation and experience can alone produce conviction. The weak point of dogmatism is that it attempts to teach that which can only be learned from life itself. His children had not shared in his life, and it was now of little avail to recount it to them, in all its details, or to explain the motives that directed it. There was enough of contradiction implied in the fact that the father was obliged to tell what his life had been.

In his own mind, Eberhard acknowledged that his own conduct had borne its legitimate results. He had no real claim to filial affection; at all events, not to the degree in which he craved it, for he had lived for himself alone. When Irma returned and asked permission to visit her friend Emma, he nodded assent. He had boasted that nothing could interrupt him. He might use the rule for himself, but not for others. He had told his child the story of his life--who knew but what this untoward interruption would efface it all from her memory?

CHAPTER XI

Seated in the open court carriage, Irma rode over hill and dale. She lay back on the cushions; the waiting-maid and the lackey sat on the back seat.

Emma's sad and sudden message had almost paralyzed her; but, now that she was in the carriage, her strength returned. Travel and change of air always exerted a magic influence over her.

The echo of her father's story followed her during a great part of the journey. She had listened with great interest, although the story itself had made but a faint impression upon her. An inner voice told her: These matters are not so serious or important as he takes them. It is his peculiar temperament that causes them to affect his course in life. It would not be so with another. It was enough that she was able to do justice to his eccentricity. He could hardly expect it to exert any decided influence upon her. Emma's fate was horrible, maddening; but her father's was not. Much of his life-trouble was mere self-torment. He spoke of repose, and yet knew it not.

With all Irma's affection for her father, she had really so little in common with him, that the painful expression that played about his mouth, while he told her his story, simply served to remind her of the Laocoön.

Irma shook her head quite petulantly.

What a chaos is the world!

A mad dog destroys a life and, here and there, solitary beings are tormenting themselves to death. Every one is conscious of some fault or weakness; all seek the unattainable and, in unending attempts and trials, life is spent. In the midst of this chaos, a single figure appears. It is full, beautiful, great, sure of life and, in truth, controls life. Irma turned back as if to say: "Alas! it is not you, father, although you could and ought to be the one. The king alone is the one free being on the pinnacle of life."

A smile played about her lips while she thought of him. She looked up at the blue heavens and, forgetting whither she was going, felt as if gentle arms were carrying her away over hill and dale.

An eagle was winging its flight far above the mountain tops. Irma's eyes followed it for a long while. She ordered the driver to stop the carriage, and the servant alighted in order to receive her ladyship's order. She motioned him to mount the box again, and, though all the comforts wealth affords were hers, stopped in the midst of wild nature to watch the eagle hovering in the air, until it at last disappeared in the clouds.

"If one must die, I'd like to die thus," said an inner voice, "fly into heaven and be no more."

They drove on. For the rest of the journey, Irma did not utter a word. It was toward evening when the lackey said: "We've reached the place."

The road descended toward the lake, by the shore of which the carriage stopped. The convent was on an island in the center of the lake, and the sounds of the curfew bells filled the air. The sun was still visible over the mountain tops, its rays were almost horizontal, and the dancing, sparkling waves looked like so many lights swimming to and fro. The surface of the lake was rapidly assuming a golden hue.

At the sound of the evening bells, the lackey and the postilion lifted their hats and the waiting-maid folded her hands. Irma also folded her hands, but did not pray. She thought to herself: The sound of the bells is pleasant enough, if one can listen to them from without, and then return to the happy world; but to those who are within the convent, it is a daily death-knell; for life such as theirs, is death.

Irma's mood was not in sympathy with that of her friend, and she did her best to feel as befitted the occasion.

While they were getting the boat ready, she overheard the lackey speaking with another servant whose face she remembered to have seen at court.

She heard the court lackey saying:

"My master's been here for some days and has been waiting for something; I don't know what."

Irma would have liked to ask with whom he had come, but a sudden fear overpowered her and she was unable to speak a word.

Accompanied by the waiting-maid, she stepped into the boat. An old boatman and his daughter rowed the rudderless skiff. The waters of the lake were deep and dark. The sun was setting, and the shadows of the western mountains were reflected in dark outlines on the hills along the shore. The fresh-fallen snow lay on the glaciers, whose white crests contrasted sharply with the wooded hills of the foreground and the clear blue sky. Below, all was as silent and dusky as though they were sailing into the realm of shadows.

"Is this your daughter?" asked Irma, addressing the old boatman.

He nodded a glad assent, delighted to find her conversant with the dialect of that portion of the country. Her intercourse with Walpurga had kept her in practice.

"Yes," replied the boatman, "and she'd like to go into service with some good family. She can sew well and--"

"Remain with your father; that's the best thing you can do," said Irma to the girl.

They rowed on in silence. "How deep is the lake here?" inquired Irma.

"Sixty fathoms, at least." Irma's hand played with the water, and she was pleased with the thought that human beings could so easily and boldly move along over a threatening, watery grave. She leaned a little way over the side of the boat, and the boatman called out:

"Take care, miss!"

"I can swim," replied Irma, splashing the waves.

"That's all very well," said the old man, laughing. "They can all swim until they have to, and then all's over; and if they happen to have clothes hanging to them, mighty few can swim."

"You're right there. Our gay frippery would drag us down."

The old man did not understand her and made no reply.

She was quite excited and asked: "Have many persons been drowned in this lake?"

"Very few; but just below us, there's the body of a young man, twenty-one years old."

"How was he lost?"

"They say he'd been drinking too freely, but I think that he had a sweetheart in the convent over there. It's a good thing she don't know of it."

Irma looked down into the waves, while the old man continued:

"And over there by the rock the trunk of a tree struck a woodcutter and hurled him into the lake. Over there by the flood-gate, a milkmaid, fifteen years old, happened to get into the current where the drift logs were whirling along, and by the time her body reached the lake, every bit of clothing had been torn from it by the logs."

"Don't tell such frightful stories," said the waiting-maid to the man.

Irma looked up at the steep mountains and asked:

"Could one climb up there?"

"Yes, but they'd find it mighty hard work; still, wherever there are trees, man can climb."

Irma looked down into the lake, and then up at the mountains. One can lose one's-self in the world. "How would it be if one were to do so?" said the voice within her.

She stood up in the boat. The old man exclaimed:

"Sit down! there's danger if you stir one way or the other."

"I shall not move," said Irma, and she really stood erect in the unsteady little boat.

"By your leave, the beautiful young lady surely doesn't mean to enter the convent?"

"Why do you ask?"

"Because I'd be sorry."

"Why would you be sorry? Don't the nuns lead a pleasant, peaceful life?"

"Oh, yes, they do; but it is a life in which nothing happens."

As if obeying a higher summons, Irma sat down and immediately stood up again. The boat reeled.

"A life in which nothing happens"--the words touched a chord in her own heart. With her, the pride and strength of youth rebelled against sacrificing one's life in such a manner. It is a life in which nothing happens: whether it be, like her father's, spent in solitary thought, or, like that of the nun's, in common devotion. Are we not placed upon earth so that we may call all our own--come joy, come grief; come mirth, come sadness--a life in which nothing happens is not for me.

Filled with such thoughts she stepped ashore and, while walking up the avenue of lindens that led to the convent, heard the boatman fastening his skiff by the chain.

She inquired for Sister Euphrosyne. The nuns were all at vespers. Irma also repaired to the chapel, in which the everlasting lamp was the only light. Although the service was over, the sisters were still kneeling on the floor. At last they arose, looking like so many ghostly figures stepping out from chaotic darkness.

Irma returned to the parlor, where the portress told her that she would not be allowed to speak to Emma that day, as the sisters were not permitted to receive any communication, or converse with any one, after vespers. Irma, in the mean while, was lodged in the convent.

It was a mild September night. Wrapped in her plaid, Irma sat out on the landing until a late hour. Her thoughts were lost in the illimitable. She scarcely knew what she was thinking of, and yet, as if wafted toward her on the air, she would now and then seem to hear the words: "A life in which nothing happens."

On the following morning, after early mass, Irma was permitted to visit her friend. She was frightened when she saw Emma, and yet it was the same mild countenance, only terribly disfigured by the closely fitting hood that completely covered the hair and gave her face greater prominence.

After the first outburst of grief and sympathy that followed the recital of her sad affliction, Emma at last said to Irma, who had again and again pressed her to her heart:

"Your embraces are so passionate. I know you will never be able to learn humility. You cannot; it is not your nature. But you should acquire equanimity. You could never enter a convent, Irma, and never ought to; or you would long to return to the world. You must become a good wife, but do not imagine that your ideal will ever be realized. Our existence here is fragmentary and full of misery. Life here below is not intended to be beautiful and complete. But, Irma, take heed you do not attempt to loosen a barrier, or to overstep it. Draw back while you are still on this side!"

Emma did not mention the king's name. There was a long pause. Irma felt as if their present surroundings must stifle her.

Emma spoke of what had happened but a few weeks ago, as if decades has passed in the mean while. She discoursed to her friend the strength that lay in continuous devotion; how it lengthened the hours into years full of placid victory over the world. She felt happy that it was possible, even on earth, to lay aside one's name and memories, and lead an existence which, without one steep step, gradually led one to eternal bliss. Emma, however, complained that they would not allow her to take the veil, and resented it as tyranny that she was only permitted to remain as a serving sister without vows.

"It is right that you should not," exclaimed Irma; "I think Bronnen loves you, but he's a man who respects existing facts. His moral character would lead him to repress, rather than manifest, warm feeling toward an affianced bride. He deserves you. I don't say that you should now--How could you? How would he dare? You should remain your own mistress and, after you've spent a year or more in the convent, you may, with that excellent man, lead a life which, if void of transports, will be none the less true and beautiful. All I can say to you now is: Don't fetter your future. No one should take a vow that binds him for life, that, on the very morrow, might seal his lips and make him a slave, a liar, a hypocrite or a deceiver, in his own eyes."

"Irma," exclaimed Emma, "what bad advice are you giving me. Is that the language used at court? Oh, forgive me for speaking to you so! It was the old Emma that did it; not I. Forgive me, I pray you, forgive me!"

She threw herself on her knees at Irma's feet.

"Stand up," said Irma, "I've nothing to forgive. I will speak more calmly. You see, dear Emma, it is fortunate for you that you cannot take the vow. A fearful blow has prostrated you; but if you remain free in your seclusion, your load will gradually lighten and your wounds will heal. Then, should the world call you, you are free to return to it. This should be a place of refuge for you, and not a prison."

"Ah yes," said Emma, with a smile, "you must of course think so, but I--I do not care to see the world again which no longer contains him who was dearer to me than life. You cannot realize what it is to be betrothed on earth, and be obliged to wait for eternal union in heaven. I have prayed God to take my heart from me and banish every selfish desire, and He has hearkened unto me. It is tyrannical to attempt to force our opinions upon others. Do you still remember, Irma, the first time we read the story of Odysseus, and how he had them bind him to the mast so that he might listen to the songs of the syrens and yet not be able to follow them? Do you still remember the remark you then made?"

"I've quite forgotten it."

"'Much-bepraised Odysseus,' said you, 'was a weakling, not a hero. A hero must not suffer himself to be bound by external fetters; he must resist everything by his inner strength.' Even then, I felt how strong you were. Odysseus was only a heathen and knew nothing of the eternal law. I rejoice in that law; I cling to that rock. I long for the divine, the eternal bond; it will support me if I sink. I do not wish to return to the world. I wish to fetter myself, and can it be that men who claim to be free dare forbid others to tread the path that leads to perfection--to the true eternal life? Is not that tyrannical and godless?"

"Yes; but who forbids you?"

"The law of the state. It has ordered this convent to be closed and forbids its taking any more young nuns."

"And does the law say that?"

"Yes."

"The king shall not allow it."

Irma spoke so loudly that her words were echoed back from the vaulted ceiling of the cell.

Emma's glance was fastened on Irma--if it only could be brought about!

The two maidens had no time to exchange a word on the subject, for, at that moment, the abbess sent for them.

The abbess addressed Irma, just as if she had overheard the last words of the latter. With gentle voice, but positive manner, she complained of the tyranny of the free-thinkers--whom she did not judge, but simply pitied--and maintained that the attempt to destroy ancient and holy institutions was revolting.

Irma's countenance glowed with excitement. She again said that the law must be repealed, and that she would exert all her influence to bring about that end. She offered to write to the king at once. The abbess gladly accepted the proffered service and Irma wrote:

"*Your Majesty*: I write to you from the convent, but I am not a nun. I believe my talent does not lie in that way. But what laws are these that forbid a maiden from taking the eternal vow? Is that freedom? Is it justice? What is it? Your Majesty will, I trust, pardon my agitation. I am writing with convent ink on convent paper, and it is not the first time that such ink and such paper have been used in the service of freedom.

"Is it possible that one set of human beings can forbid others to live together in seclusion?

"Quacks cannot create life or happiness; should they, therefore, be allowed to forbid unhappiness from effecting its own cure?

"Your Majesty's great mind cannot suffer such barbarism, and it is barbarous, although hedged about by culture.

"I am aware, Your Majesty, that I have not yet made my meaning clear. I shall endeavor to do so.

"I am here in the convent.

"Emma, the woman whom I love above all others--I believe I have already spoken of her to Your Majesty--wishes to take the veil. From her point of view, she is in the right. Dogs will go mad, although the dog-tax be paid. A mad dog killed her affianced and she now desires to renounce the world. Who dare prevent it? And yet the law of the state commands that this convent shall die out, and forbids its receiving nuns.

"Your Majesty dare not permit this. Your eye takes in all at a glance; your life is the nation's history. You must teach these journeymen to be greater-minded than they now are. They must abolish this law; indeed, they must.

"Pardon my language. Your Majesty; but I cannot help myself. I feel as if I were your deputy. I feel that your great mind resents such pettiness as an insult.

"I hope to see Your Majesty soon again, and, meanwhile, send my most respectful greetings.

"Irma von Wildenort."

Without being observed, Irma inclosed the four-petaled clover-leaf with the letter.

While Irma sat in the boat that took her back to the shore, she was filled with pride. She felt that she had instigated, if not accomplished, a beautiful and noble act in the service of freedom and was determined that it should be carried out.

The old boatman was glad to see her again. He rowed lustily, but did not speak a word. Now and then, he would smile to himself, as if happy in the thought that he was carrying a young soul away from the realm of shadows.

In the distance there was a skiff and, in it, a man clad in a green hunting dress. He waved his hat and bowed.

Absorbed in thought, Irma was gazing into the lake, when her maid drew her attention to the other boat.

Irma started.

"Is it not the king?"

Thinking that he had not yet been observed, the hunter fired off his gun, the report of which was echoed again and again from the hills. He then waved his hat once more. With trembling hand, Irma waved her white handkerchief as a token of recognition.

The skiff approached. Irma's expression rapidly changed from one of joy to that of disappointment.

It was not the king. It was Baron Schoning who greeted her.

He sprang into the boat, kissed her trembling hand and told her how happy he was to meet her there.

They alighted. The baron offered his arm to Irma and they walked along the bank, the maid going before. In the distance, Irma could see the lackey who, on the previous day, had been speaking to hers. Had not the servant said that his master had been waiting here for a long time? Had not Baron Schoning, before this, been open in his attentions to her? His words soon relieved her of all doubt on that score.

"We are alone here, in the presence only of the mountains, the lake and the heavens. Dearest Countess! May I speak of something that lies near my heart and which I have for a long while desired to tell you?"

She silently nodded assent.

"Well then, permit me to tell you that the court is not the right place for you."

"I am not quite sure that I shall return there; but why do you think me out of place there?"

"Because there is something in you which will always prevent you from feeling at home there. You are surprised to hear me, the jester, the court warbler, speak thus. I know very well I bear that title; but believe me, Countess, while they imagine they are playing with me, I am amusing myself at their expense. You, Countess, will never feel at home at court. You do not accept that life and its customs, as fixed and settled. You interpret it according to your own peculiar views; your mind cannot wear a uniform; your soul utters its deepest feelings in its own dialect, and when your utterances get abroad in the liveried world, they find it exceedingly original, but strange and--no one knows it better than I--you have not, and never will have aught in common with those who surround you."

"I should not have believed that you could thus look into my heart; but I thank you."

"I am not looking into your heart; I live in it. Oh, Countess! Oh! thou child-like and all-loving heart, tremble not! Suffer me to clasp this hand in mine, while I tell you that I, too, am a stranger there, and have resolved to retire from court and live for myself on yonder patrimonial estate of mine. Irma, will you render my life a thousand-fold happier than it can otherwise be? Will you be my wife?"

It was long before Irma could answer him. At last she said:

"My friend--yes, my friend--on yonder island there lives a friend of mine who is dead, both to herself and me. Fate deals kindly with me and sends me another in her stead. I thank you--but--I am so confused--perhaps more than-- But look, dear baron, at the little cottage half-way up the mountain. I would be content to live there--to grow my cabbages, milk my goats, plant my hemp, make my clothes--and could be happy, desiring nothing, forgetting the world and forgotten by it."

"You jest, dear Countess; you are creating an idea whose bright colors will soon grow dim."

"I do not jest. I could live alone while laboring for my daily bread, but not as the mistress of a castle and surrounded by the trifles and frippery of the fashionable world. To dress for the mere sake of seeing one's self in the glass, is not to my taste. In yonder cottage, I could live without a mirror. I need not look at myself, nor need another look at me; but if I am to live with the world, I must be wholly with it; at the reigning center, in the metropolis, or traveling. I must have all or nothing. Nothing else will make me happy. Nothing half-and-half or intermediate will satisfy me."

Irma's tone was so determined that the baron saw how thoroughly in earnest she was, and that her words meant more than mere caprice or sport.

"I must either subject myself to the world," said she, "or, despising it, put it beneath me. I must either be perfectly indifferent and regardless of the impression I produce upon others, or else afraid of every glance, even my own."

The baron was silent, and evidently at a loss for words.

At last he said:

"I would gladly have gone to your father's house, but I know that he dislikes men of my class. I waited for you here, knowing that you would come to your friend. Pray answer me another question: Do you intend to return to court?"

"Yes," said Irma, now, for the first time, firmly resolved upon returning. "It were ungrateful to act otherwise. Ungrateful to the queen and to--the king and all my friends. I feel sure, my friend, that I am not yet mature enough to lead a life in which nothing happens."

They came to a seat.

"Will you not sit down with me?" said Irma to the baron.

They seated themselves.

"When did you leave the capital?"

"Five days ago."

"And was everything going on as usual?"

"Alas, not everything. Doctor Gunther has met with a sad affliction. Professor Korn, his son-in-law, died suddenly, having poisoned himself while dissecting a corpse."

"While dissecting a corpse?" exclaimed Irma. "We all die of the poison of decay, but not so suddenly; those on yonder island and we--all of us."

"You are very bitter."

"Not at all. My head is filled with the strangest fancies. I became acquainted with a great law over there.

"The law of renunciation?"

"Oh, no; the justification of fashion."

"You are mocking."

"By no means. Fashion is the charter of human liberty and the journal of fashion is humanity's greatest boon."

"What an odd conceit!"

"Not at all. It is the simple truth. The frequency with which a man changes the material, cut and color of his clothes, proves his claim to culture. It is man alone who constantly clothes himself differently and anew. The tree retains its bark, the animal its hide, and, as the national and clerical costumes are both stereotyped, as it were, those who use them are regarded as belonging to an inferior, or less civilized class."

The baron looked at Irma, wonderingly. He was glad at heart, that she had candidly given him the mitten. He could not have satisfied so restless and exacting a nature that constantly required intellectual fireworks for its amusement; and she, moreover, took delight in her absurd ways. All at once, he saw nothing but the shadows in Irma's character. An hour ago, he had seen only the bright side and had regarded her as a vision of light itself. She had just visited a friend about to take the veil, had just listened to a proposal of marriage--how could she possibly indulge in such strange notions immediately afterward?

Baron Schoning told her that he had ordered photographs of Walpurga and the prince.

"Ah, Walpurga," said Irma, as if suddenly remembering something.

The baron politely took his leave and rowed back across the lake.

Irma took the road that led homeward. She wished to visit Walpurga's relatives and inquired as to the route toward the lake on the other side of the mountains. They told her that a carriage could not get there, and that the only way to reach the point was on horseback. Irma took the direct road for home.

CHAPTER XII

"Something ails me! It always seems as if some one were calling me, and I can't help looking round to see who it is. The countess must be thinking of us all the time. Ah me, she's the best creature in the world."

Whilst Walpurga, for many days, thus lamented Irma's departure, the others at the palace rarely thought of her. The place we leave, be it to journey in this or to the other world, is speedily filled. In the palace, they tolerate neither vacancies nor sentiment. There, life is a part of history; and history, as we all know, never stands still.

Mademoiselle Kramer continued to teach Walpurga how to write, and the latter did not understand her, when she said: "The quality are fond of taking up all sorts of things, but we must finish what we begin. I've finished many a piece of embroidery, of which the hand that was kissed for it scarcely worked a couple of stitches; but that's in the order of things."

Although Mademoiselle Kramer found everything in order that was done by the quality, she, nevertheless, had a habit of speaking of such things to her inferiors, not with the hope of being understood by them, but merely to relieve her mind.

The child was well and hearty. Day after day passed in quiet routine, and now Walpurga was richly recompensed for the absence of Countess Irma. The queen was permitted to have the nurse and child about her for several hours every day.

While Irma had gone forth to seek rest and quiet, but had found chaos instead, the queen's life had become serene and happy; Her recent experience of life's trials had been a novel and difficult one; but now her mind was at rest, her health restored. She would look at her child and, when she spoke, Walpurga would fold her hands and listen in silence. The nurse did not understand all that was said, but, nevertheless, sympathized with what was going on. The queen endeavored to console Doctor Gunther in his affliction, and spoke to him of the consolation that the mother could find in her child: "In spite of all life's contradictions and enigmas," said she "there is yet the one glad thought that every child bears within it the possibility of the highest human development."

The queen while speaking looked around at her child, and Walpurga said in a gentle voice:

"Look at our child; it's laughing for the first time. It's seven weeks old to-day."

"I've seen my child's first smile, and its father is not here."

"Don't make such a long face," said Walpurga; "just keep on laughing and he'll laugh too; your pleasant glances will bide in his face."

The child kept smiling until the doctor requested them not to excite it any more. He said that Walpurga was right and that if one looks at an infant kindly it has the effect of imprinting a sweet expression upon its features.

From that day forward the child never saw a sad look on its mother's face.

It was only when she spoke of persons that Walpurga could talk volubly and continuously. Countess Irma was therefore frequently the topic of conversation. But this subject was soon exhausted, and when the queen would say: "Why are you silent? I hear that you can talk to the child so prettily and carry on all sorts of fun with him," Walpurga persistently remained silent.

The queen made Walpurga tell her her history. It required much questioning to get at the entire story for Walpurga could not narrate it in a continuous strain as she had never thought of her life as a connected whole. Everything had gone on of its own accord as it were and without requiring one to stop and think. While telling her story she was as anxious as if before a court of justice.

"How did you happen to fall in love with your husband? Do you love him with all your heart?"

"Of course. He's my husband and there isn't a bad drop of blood in him. He's a little awkward--I mean unhandy,--but only when others are about. He's never been much among people. He grew up in a one-storied house and until he was twenty-two years old had seen nothing but trees; but no work's too hard for him and whatever you put him to, he does his duty. He's not so dull, either; but he doesn't show it to the world; with me, he can talk well enough, and he's satisfied as long as I know he's the right sort of man. It takes my Hansei a long while to make up his mind, but when he's made it up, he's always right. You see, dear queen, I might have got a much cleverer husband; my playmate was a hunter, and his comrade was after me for a long while; but I didn't want to have anything to do with him, for he's too much in love with himself. He once rowed over the lake with me, and was all the time looking at himself in the water, and twisting his mustache and making mouths, and so thought I to myself: If your clothes were made of gold, I wouldn't have you. And when father was drowned in the lake, Hansei was at hand and did everything about the house. He'd go out in his skiff and bring in fish, and while I and mother would sell 'em, he'd work in the forest. Father was also woodcutter and fisherman, at the same time. And so Hansei was there a full half year; no one bid him come and no one told him to go, for he was there and was honest and good and never gave me an unkind word; and so we were married, and, thank God, we're happy and, through our good prince, we'll have something of our own. We've got it already, and it's no easy matter for a husband to give his wife away for a year. But Hansei didn't waste many words over it. If a thing's right and must be, he only nods--this way--and then it's done. Forgive me, dear queen, for telling you all this silly stuff, but you asked me."

"No, I am heartily glad that there are simple-minded, happy beings in this world. The worldly-wise think they prove their infinite wisdom when they say: 'There are no simple-minded, happy people, and the country folk are not nearly so good as we imagine.'"

"No more they are," said Walpurga, eagerly; "there aren't any worse people than some of those out our way. There are good ones, of course; but there are wicked and envious and thieving and lazy and good-for-nothing and godless creatures besides; and Zenza and Thomas are among the worst, but I can't help it."

Walpurga imagined that the queen must know of the pardon, and they should not say of her that she had not told the truth. The queen felt grieved at Walpurga's vehemence and the serious charges she made against the people of her neighborhood.

After a little while, she said to Walpurga:

"They tell me you sing so beautifully. Sing something for me, or, rather, for the child."

"No, dear queen, I can't do it. I'd like to, but I can't. I don't know any but silly songs. The good ones are all church songs."

"Sing me one of those that you call silly songs."

"No, I can't; they're lonely songs."

"What do you mean by lonely songs?"

"I don't know, but that's what they call 'em."

"Ah, I understand: they can only be sung when one is solitary and alone."

"Yes, I suppose that's it; the queen's right."

Although the queen endeavored to induce her to sing, Walpurga protested that she could not and finally became so agitated that she burst into tears. The queen experienced some difficulty in pacifying her, but succeeded at last, and then Walpurga, taking the child with her, returned to her room.

On the following day Walpurga was again summoned to the queen, who said: "You're right, Walpurga. You can't sing to me. I've been thinking a great deal about you. The bird on the tree doesn't sing at one's bidding. Free nature cannot be directed by a baton. You needn't sing for me. I shall not ask it of you again."

Walpurga had intended to sing to the queen that day. She had chosen her prettiest songs and now the queen actually ordered her not to sing, and even compared her to a bird. "Palace folk," thought she, "are queer folk."

"I understand," continued the queen, "that in your neighborhood they believe in the Lady of the Lake. Do you believe in her, too?"

"Believe in her? I don't know, but they tell of her. Father saw her three days before he died, and that was a sure sign that he would soon die. They say, too, that she's the Lady of Waldeck."

"Who is the Lady of Waldeck?"

"She's the Lady of Wörth."

"What is Wörth?"

"A bit of land in the middle of the lake, with water all round it."

"Do you mean an island?"

"Yes, an island; we sometimes call it that, too.

"And what is the story of the Lady of Waldeck?"

"Once upon a time, many thousand years ago, there was a man, and he was a knight by the name of Waldeck, and he was a crusader. He and lots of emperors and kings went off to our Saviour's grave in the Holy Land. He left his wife at home and before he went away, he said to her: 'You're good and you'll remain true to me'; and when, after many years, he returned, quite black with the eastern sun, he found his wife with another man, and so he bound the two together, put them in a boat and rowed them over to Wörth where he left them; and there they lay, and had nothing to eat, and nothing to drink, and were tied together and died of hunger, and the birds of the air ate them. They were adulterers and it served them right; but he was horrible for all. And even nowadays, on spirit nights, you can often see a little blue flame on the island of Wörth, and they say that the Lady of Waldeck's soul has passed into a nymph and that she must wander about."

Such was Walpurga's story.

"I haven't frightened you, I hope?" said she, anxiously, as she observed the queen's fixed gaze. "That's what they say. But may be it's only talk, after all."

"No, no. Don't be anxious about that," cried the queen. "So many different thoughts pass through my mind."

"Like enough; it's very hard to be the housewife, with so big a house as this to keep, and so many folk in it."

The queen laughed heartily.

Walpurga did not know that she had said anything odd or droll and was therefore surprised at the effect of her remarks; but she soon became satisfied that all she said was quoted. This made her quite shy, although she would now and then give way to fits of extravagance and would, at such moments, delight in her own odd freaks, for they always provoked a smile. While the queen aimed to be as simple as possible in her intercourse with Walpurga, the latter was, with each succeeding day, becoming more artificial and affected. She copied herself and her whilom *naïvete*. When she knew that the queen was within hearing, she would repeat the wondrous combination of words with which she was wont to amuse the prince. She one day began to sing of her own accord and, when she had finished, she felt surprised and almost hurt, because her song had elicited no remark from the queen. Had she not sung well?

The queen had said nothing, because she feared that she might embarrass her.

There was a strange contrast between these two women, each of whom was trying to place herself in more perfect sympathy with the other, while both were, with every step, adding to the distance that separated them.

It was a great day when the queen, accompanied by Walpurga and the crown prince, rode out for the first time.

"You're a thousand times more beautiful when you're out-of-doors, in the open air. In the darkened rooms, I never knew how beautiful you were," said Walpurga to the queen, who immediately afterward had something to say in French to the Countess Brinkenstein who sat beside her.

"May I ask a favor, gracious queen?" said Walpurga.

"Certainly. What is it?"

"I think it hurts the child to talk gibberish before it. A young soul like his understands, even if it can't speak, and it seems to me it must confuse his little brain. I hardly know how to tell you; but I feel it in my own head, and whatever affects me, affects the child."

"She's right," said the queen to Countess Brinkenstein, "until the child can speak perfectly, it should hear no language but its mother tongue."

"That's it--mother tongue," exclaimed Walpurga, "you've hit it. I had it on my lips, but I couldn't think of it; that's the very word. I'm, so to say, the same as a mother to the child and so--isn't it so?"

"Yes, certainly. It shall be as you say in all things. See to it, my dear Brinkenstein, that after this, nothing but German be spoken before the prince. No one can tell what sounds may sink into the soul which, as yet, is but half awakened."

Walpurga was delighted. There would now be no more gibberish when she was by for wherever the child was, there was she.

Mademoiselle Kramer added to her happiness by informing her that they would start for the country, that is, the summer palace, within a few days.

CHAPTER XIII

In the mean while there was a special reason for detaining Walpurga and the prince in the city.

Baron Schoning had spoken of the matter, while at breakfast one day, and the suggestion which had been offered as a bit of pleasantry was well received. The millions who were anxious to behold their future ruler were to be gratified by the work of an instant. It was determined that there should be a photograph of the crown prince borne aloft on the hands of the people, Walpurga representing the people. She urged various objections to the idea, and said it was wrong to let a child less than a year old look into a mirror, and quite wrong to have its likeness taken. "As long as you haven't let a child look in the glass, it can see itself in the hollow of its left hand." Finding that her opposition was of no avail, she dressed herself in her best gown. The crown prince looked very pretty, and as he already had fair curly hair, the artist removed his cap.

The first few attempts to get the likeness were failures. Whenever she heard the voice issuing from the dark room, Walpurga was frightened and imagined that witchery was going on. She became more and more agitated, but at last, at Schoning's clever suggestion, a pianist in the adjoining room played the air of Walpurga's favorite song. As soon as she heard it, she could not help joining in the strain. Her expression--and that of the child, too--became cheerful and unconstrained. Eureka! the picture was a success.

The drives about the city had been lovely, but the most beautiful of all was now to come.

It was a bright, balmy afternoon when they drove off. Although there had been no rain for some time, the road was free from dust, sprinklers having preceded the court carriage.

Walpurga was in an open carriage, with the prince and the queen. It was the first time that she rode out among the villages and the fields. She gazed at the people who were looking out of the windows, or sitting at the doorsteps of the houses by the roadside, at the children who would stop and salute them, and then, again, at the laborers in the fields. She kept smiling, nodding and winking in all directions. The queen asked:

"What ails you? What's the matter?"

"Oh, pardon me, queen; but here I'm riding in a carriage and four, and over there the likes of me are working and toiling, and I know how the women's backs ache from digging up potatoes, and while I ride by, as though I were somebody better than they, it makes me feel as if I ought to ask 'em all to forgive me for riding by in this way. I feel as if I ought to say: 'Never mind; when the year's over, I'll be the same as you are; the clothes I wear, the carriage and the horses, none of 'em are mine; they're all borrowed.' Ah, dear queen, forgive me for saying this to you, but you understand everything and know how to explain it for the best. I empty my whole heart out to you," said Walpurga, smiling.

"Yes, I understand what you mean," replied the queen; "and it is wise of you thus to look forward to a return to your home. The thought that you might be unable to content yourself there, has often troubled me. Believe me, we who ride in carriages are no better off than those who are walking barefoot through yonder stubble."

"I know it," said Walpurga. "No one can eat more than his fill, as my father used to say, and queens must bear their children in pain and sorrow, just like the rest of us; no one can save them from that."

The queen made no reply, and looked out of the other side of the carriage.

Countess Brinkenstein motioned Walpurga to be silent; for, while it was difficult to induce her to talk, when she had once begun, she did not know when to stop.

The queen was only silent because she wished to say something in French, to Countess Brinkenstein, and had refrained from doing so on account of Walpurga's precious admonition.

"My dear child," said the queen at last, "I would, gladly, give up everything, if I knew that I could thereby render mankind happy and contented. But what good would it do! Money wouldn't help the people, and it is not we who have brought about this inequality. God has ordained it thus."

Walpurga could easily have answered her, but thought it best to leave something for the morrow; for her father had often said: "It isn't well to catch all the fish in one day." She therefore remained silent.

The queen felt greatly constrained by her promise not to speak French in Walpurga's presence. There was much that she desired to say and with which the peasant woman had no concern.

"How beautiful! how lovely is the world," she murmured to herself, and then closed her eyes, as if fatigued with the splendor which had opened before them, after her long seclusion. And while she lay there, her head thrown back on the cushion, she looked like a sleeping angel, so peaceful, so tender, as if mother and child in one.

"The soft cushions almost make me think I am sitting on clouds," said Walpurga, when they reached their journey's end.

She was unspeakably happy in the country. The broad prospect, the clear skies, the mountains, the large and beautiful garden with its comfortable seats, the fountains, the swans--all delighted her. There was also a fine dairy-farm, about a quarter of a mile distant, where the cow-stable was much finer than the dancing floor at the Chamois inn.

Walpurga was out in the open air during the greater part of the day. The queen lived for her child alone, and Walpurga was again talkative and natural. All the affected ways that she had acquired while in the city, had left her.

In her first letter home--she could now write for herself--she said: "If I only had you here for one day, to tell you about everything; for, if the sky were nothing but paper and our lake nothing but ink, I couldn't write it all. If it were only not so far off, Hansei; a pound of fish here costs twice as much as with us. We're living in the summer palace now, and just think, mother, what such a king has. He has seven palaces, and they're all furnished, every one with a hundred beds, rooms, kitchens and all of them filled, and when they go from one palace to another they needn't take a fork or a spoon along. Everything here is silver, and the doctor and the apothecary and the preacher and the court people and the horses and the carriages, all move out here with us. There's a whole town here in the palace, and I've the best beer and more than I care for; and when one gets up in the morning everything is as neat and clean as a new-laid egg. There's not a leaf on the paths, and then there's a house all made with glass. The flowers live in it; but I daren't go in, because it's too hot in there. They keep it heated the whole year round, and it's filled with great palms and other trees from the east, and, in the pond, there's a fountain, and the water rises up as high as our church steeple. And just think of all such a king can have. All day long, when the sun shines, there's a rainbow there, sometimes above and sometimes below. Of course, he nor no one else can make the sun; and they all do their best to please me. I hardly can say I like a thing, before they give it to me at once.

"The queen is just like a companion with me. Just like you, Stasi. I wish you much joy at your wedding. I only heard of it from Zenza. You shall have a wedding present from me; let me know what you'd like to have. But now I beg of you, just tell me how it goes with my child. It didn't please me to know that you had weighed it on the butcher's scales, and that it's so heavy. I wouldn't have thought, mother, that you would have allowed it, or that you, Hansei, would have given way to the innkeeper. Beware of that fellow. It was only last night that I dreamt you and he were rowing across the lake, and that he clutched you and dragged you into the water. Then all was over. And then the Lady of the Lake appeared, and she looked like the good countess who is now away. She's the best friend I have here, and promised to visit you on her way back. You can tell her and give her everything just as if it was myself. They've just brought me my dinner. Ah, dear mother, if I could only give you some of it. There are so many good things here and there's always so much left. Don't let yourself want for anything, or Hansei either, and my child least of all, for we can now afford it, thank God! And I want to be with you for a long while yet, dear mother. It often makes me feel bad that I can't be a mother--I mean a true mother; but when I come home I'll make it all up to my child; and Hansei, put all your money out at interest until I get home; remember, it doesn't belong to us, but to our child, whom we deprive of its mother.

"Mademoiselle Kramer, who is with me all day, was born here. She'd rather be in the city, and she says it used to be much prettier here than it now is; that everything used to be like the little garden yonder, where there are walls and rooms with doors and windows, all made of shrubbery. It's all very pretty and I like to go there, but when I've been there a few minutes I am almost frightened to death: for I feel as if I and the trees were bewitched, and I get away as soon as I can. Mademoiselle Kramer is a very good person, but nothing is quite to her taste. She's been used all her life to riding and fine eating and sitting about; and mother, just think of what I have eaten here--live ice! People here are so clever they can preserve ice and make it up so that you can eat it. Yes, if that could satisfy one's appetite, there wouldn't be any hungry people with us in the winter, or even in the summer, further up the mountains. And mother, you once told me a fairy-tale about walls that have ears; but this is no fable, it's true and quite natural. They have speaking-trumpets, running through the whole palace, and you can speak through them, and if I want anything in my room, all I've got to do is to go up to the wall and say so and in a minute it's there.

"This is a beautiful day and that makes me think that you have it as well as we, and that the same sun that shines on us here shines on you, too.

"The main business here is taking walks. Every one must take walks here. They call it taking exercise, so that they can get up their appetite and keep their limbs from getting stiff. They even take the horses out walking when there's nothing for them to do. Early in the morning, the grooms ride out a long way with them and then come home. I often wish the horses could only take me home for an hour. I often get homesick, but I am well and hearty and only hope it is the same with you. Your

"Walpurga.

"Postscript.--Why haven't you mentioned a word about the little gold heart which my countess sent to my Burgei? And no one is to send me any more petitions, or to come to me. I won't receive another one. As long as I live, I'll be sorry for having anything to do with Zenza and Thomas; but perhaps it's all for the best and may be he's turned out better. Don't think hard of it, dear Hansei, but I beg you, once more, to have very little to do with the host of the Chamois. He's a rogue, and a dangerous one at that, but you needn't tell him that I say so, for I want the ill-will of no one. I send my love to all good friends. I must stop now, my hand is quite stiff with writing.

"Stop! I must begin again. I send you a picture of myself and my prince. It was taken in a sort of peepshow, before we came out here, and now, as long as the world lasts, the prince and I will always be together, and I'll be holding him in my arms. But I am still with you, dear Hansei, and you, dear mother, and, most of all, with my dear child that I bear in my heart where no one can look. Don't show the picture to any one.

"But, dear me! what good will it do if you don't show it? Mademoiselle Kramer tells me that they've made a hundred thousand pictures of me and the prince, and now I am hanging up in all the shops, and wherever I go they know me as well as the king and the queen, whose pictures hang next to mine. I feel as if I wanted no one ever to see me again, but when I think of it, it's really an honor after all. I am out in the world now, and must let them do what they please with me.

"But I shall ever be true to you, and I am at home nowhere but with you, and am always there in thought."

CHAPTER XIV

"How goes it, Walpurga?" asked Baum, one morning, when the nurse was looking out of the window of the ground floor.

"Oh, dear," replied she, "this is a real paradise."

"Indeed!"

"Could it be any finer in paradise? The people live without care and have nothing to do but eat and drink and laugh and go out walking."

"You're right there; but still it was finer in paradise, for there father Adam couldn't covet another man's wife, as his was the only one in the world."

"What queer notions you have," said Walpurga, laughing; and Baum, feeling flattered, added:

"In paradise they had no use for servants, no coachman, no cook, no house, no clothes. There were no boots to be cleaned, because there were none, and there were no coats and shirts to be woven, and sewed and mended."

"You dreadful creature," exclaimed Walpurga. She felt as if Baum's words had almost torn the clothes from her; her face was crimson. Baum quickly answered:

"I'm sorry I look so dreadful in your eyes. In my eyes you're so beautiful that I--" He was interrupted by a servant who called him away.

Walpurga quickly drew back into the room. She was angry at Baum. How could any one use such language to a married woman? "And yet," thought she, with a self-complacent smile, "Baum's a well-mannered person, after all; and why shouldn't one crack a joke, now and then?" She looked in the large mirror for a moment and smiled.

"Yes, when Hansei sees you again, he'll hardly know you; it's the good living that does it. But I'll say to myself every day: 'It won't last long; you're only hired here for a while. But dancing's pleasant, even if the dance doesn't last long,'" said Walpurga, as if to console herself. All sort of dance tunes occurred to her and she kept humming them to the prince.

Walpurga roamed about through the beautiful park as if in a dream. She imagined that the trees, the sky and the birds were all enchanted and in a strange world; that they would suddenly awaken and all would vanish. But everything went on in its quiet course, each day as beautiful as the one that preceded, like the sun rising anew every day, the flowers that are constantly giving forth their fragrance, or the spring that never ceases to flow.

Walpurga had a special liking for Mademoiselle Kramer's father, who was governor of the castle. He was a venerable man who raised lovely flowers in his little lodge, and she could talk to him as with her own father.

Walpurga was sitting out of doors for the greater part of the day. Mademoiselle Kramer was always with her and two servants within ready call. The queen would also often join them.

The queen had a beautiful snow-white setter of which the child was especially fond. Walpurga requested her to let the prince often have the dog, because it is well for a child to have a living animal about it.

"She is right," said the queen, addressing the court lady at her side; "animal life awakens human consciousness."

Walpurga stared at her in surprise. The queen had said she was right, but added words that she did not understand.

"Just look," said she to the queen, "how fond the bees are of our child. They won't hurt him--you needn't fear. The bee is the only creature that came out of paradise without being spoiled."

The queen manifested her pleasure at the manner in which Walpurga's thoughts were, interwoven with tradition.

Walpurga observed that the queen had but little worldly wisdom and gave her the benefit of hers whenever opportunity presented itself.

"Do you know what that is?" she once asked, while they sat in the shrubbery.

"A tree."

"Yes, but do you know it's a sacred tree and that lightning doesn't strike where it grows?"

"No, I never knew that."

"And then of course, you don't know why. Now my mother told me all about it. The Virgin was once crossing a mountain and was caught in a fearful storm. So she stood under a great large hazel-tree and remained safe, and, because it had protected her she blessed it for all time. You can make magic wands from hazel twigs. The serpent-king dwells under the hazel-tree and, sometimes, under the weeping willow. Do you know why the weeping willow drops its branches so sadly?"

"No, I don't know that either. You're full of wisdom," said the queen, smiling.

"I'm not, but my mother is. I don't know half as much as she. She's very clever, and told me about the weeping willow. The rods with which they scourged our Saviour were made from the weeping willow, and ever since that time she droops her branches with shame."

Walpurga was quite happy to think that she could teach the queen something. She felt that she was quite a different being from all in the palace and that the queen was the only one who understood her. She was always happy and cheerful when with her and opened her whole heart to the queen. "You're quite a stranger in the world; you've never, in all your life, seen how the burghers and farmers sit in their rooms of an evening, what they eat, what they talk of, what they wish for, and what makes them happy or gives them pain. I once heard my father tell a story. It was about a prince and a princess who grew up as shepherds, and didn't know who they were until they were grown up, when they said to him: 'you're a prince,' and to her: 'you're a princess,' and they became right good and honest people. Of course they'd been out in the world, and had learned how people live and what they need. I only wish that we could send our prince out the same way. I think it would be good for him and the whole country, too. If servants are running after you all day long, it's just as if you were in a prison, the people form a living wall around you."

"We can all be honest and good," replied the queen.

"And make good men and women of our children," added Walpurga. "Do you know what I'd like? I'd like, as long as I live, to take all trouble from you, and if sickness came to you, to be sick in your place."

"Yes that's very well; but let us be quiet now."

The queen was all happiness. She saw to the bottom of a simple peasant woman's heart, and into a new world that revealed itself to her in her child.

CHAPTER XV

Baum availed himself of every opportunity to speak with Walpurga. He was in deep affliction; his wife was seriously ill, and Walpurga endeavored to console him. In return, Baum lent a willing ear to all her complaints, for she had just heard from home, that Zenza denied all knowledge of the little golden heart that Countess Irma had sent to the child.

"Ah, and so your countess has a golden heart left to give away," said Baum in a mocking voice. "You ought to be glad to have such a friend."

"And so I am. Oh, if she were only here again, then it would be a real paradise. I don't worry about Zenza's making away with the golden heart; there must be some bad people, or else the world would be too beautiful."

"And I tell you, it's only half a life when the king's away. Just wait till he comes back and see how it will be then. When there's no man about, it isn't a complete house."

The queen approached and Baum withdrew.

"What was that man saying to you?" asked the queen.

"We were telling each other of our troubles; he has great longing for the king and I, dear queen, have great longing for my Countess Irma."

"I long for her, too; but she has asked to have her leave of absence extended for another fortnight."

Peacefully and calmly, the days passed by. Walpurga's favorite resort was in the neighborhood of the dairy-farm; for there were cows there, and cows are the same everywhere, and don't know that they belong to the king, or that their milk is served at his table.

Walpurga remarked this one day to Baum, who had discovered that he could meet her there, and he replied:

"Oh, how clever you are; if I only had got a wife like you."

"There are dozens like me."

"Oh, not so clever as you are. You could get far in the world, if you only wanted to."

"How far should I go?" said Walpurga. "I want to go home and no farther."

"No one will think the worse of you for that, but one can make a new home."

"I don't understand you."

"I can't explain now. Countess Brinkenstein is coming. Meet me in the shrubbery behind the chapel, this evening when they're all at table, I've something good to tell you."

Walpurga had not time to reply. Baum saw Countess Brinkenstein approaching and, in a loud voice, gave the dairy inspector an order from the head cook, and then walked away quickly, respectfully saluting the countess as he passed.

Countess Brinkenstein administered a severe reproof to Mademoiselle Kramer for having allowed Walpurga to stand there with the prince, and chatter with the servants.

Mademoiselle Kramer made no reply, and only motioned Walpurga to go into the vine-clad arbor.

Walpurga was busy conjecturing what sort of advice Baum might have to give her. He knew lots of things and perhaps knew of some clever stroke, by which Hansei, her mother and the child might be brought to the palace. But Hansei wouldn't do for a lackey. Perhaps, though, they could make him court fisherman or chief woodsman of the royal forest.

When evening came, she was quite uneasy. It was not the right thing for her to have a secret meeting with any man but her husband; but, perhaps the place may be given away to-morrow, and then it would be too late. She sat by the window and looked up at the stars. Her cheeks glowed, she drew a deep breath.

"What ails you?" inquired Mademoiselle Kramer.

"I feel so warm and oppressed."

"I'll send for the doctor."

"I don't need the doctor. Just let me sit here quietly. But no; let me walk up and down in the garden for a few minutes and I'll feel better."

"The maid can go with you."

"No, I don't need any one; I'll feel better if I go alone."

"But, I beg of you, don't go too far, and come back soon. You've seen, to-day, how every misstep of yours draws reproof on me."

"Yes, I'll come back soon."

Walpurga went out at the back door. The gravel grated under her footsteps and she trod more lightly. The air was laden with the perfume of the flowers; the swans in the lake uttered a strange sound, like a deep, muffled trumpet tone; the sky sparkled with countless stars and, just as Walpurga looked up, she saw a brilliant meteor and exclaimed: "Hansei!"

In her innermost heart she wished for nothing but her husband's happiness. She stopped when she had uttered his name. She felt as if she had better return. She was a married woman and oughtn't to meet a strange man at night, even though it was by the chapel.

Something ran across the path. Was it a cat, a martin or a weasel?

"Return," said an inner voice, but she went on, nevertheless. She reached the arbor. Baum stepped forth from behind a vine-clad column. He held out both his hands to her and she offered him her own. He tried to draw her closer to him but she stood firm.

"What have you to tell me?" asked Walpurga.

"Nothing but what's good. You see, we lesser folks must help each other, and you're so much to me that I could do anything for you."

"If you can do me a good service, I shall be grateful as long as I live--I and my husband and my child. Tell me quick; I'm in a hurry."

"Then we can leave it for some other time."

"No, tell me now. What do you mean?"

"I really meant nothing at all, but you see we must always wait on others, and so I thought that we might have a quarter of an hour to ourselves. I only wanted to tell you that you are the light of my life, my happiness. When I look at you, and listen to you, I'd like to do--I don't know what, and I can't tell."

"It isn't necessary, either; and let me tell you, this is very wicked of you."

"Is it wicked that I love you to distraction?"

"Yes, and doubly wicked that you fooled me here and made me believe that you had something good to tell me."

"And so I have," said Baum, quickly; "forgive me for what I've done; if you do, I'll tell you the rest."

"Yes, I'll forgive you, but make haste."

"Well," said Baum with great composure, "it's simply this. He who stands at the manger and doesn't eat, is a fool. Do you understand me?"

"Of course; it doesn't take much to know that."

"Yes, but you don't take my meaning. A court like this is a full manger, and you'll be a great fool if you go away without having taken enough to satisfy yourself and your child for life."

"I'd like to know how that can be done. You've got to eat every day, and can't stuff yourself with enough to last for a lifetime."

"You're clever, but you might be more so. Just listen! What I mean is this. A good position, or a profitable situation, should give one a chance to make himself comfortable for life. The tenant of the dairy-farm will have to leave next spring or, at the latest, in the fall, and I think you ought to manage it with the queen and the rest of them, so that your husband should get the position, and then you could be here all your life and you and yours would be well provided for. Take my word for it, I know what the quality are. If you leave here without having secured a good situation, not a cat will remember you. But if you remain here, you'll be well taken care of to the end of your days, and the older the prince gets, the more he'll think of you; and when he becomes king, he'll provide for you, your family, your child and even your grandchildren. Is that wicked advice?"

"No; on the contrary, it's very good and I'll remember it. That, indeed, would be bread and lots of butter."

"Oh, I've never seen or heard so sensible a woman as you are. You deserve a better lot; but that can't be helped, and if you remain here, I'll often have the pleasure of seeing you and speaking a word with you, for I hope we'll be good friends; shall we not?"

"Yes, indeed, and my Hansei will also be a good friend to you. There's not a false drop of blood in his body and he's clever, too, only he's not much of a talker; and he loves me just as much as gold; he's true and kindhearted, and I won't let any one say a word against him."

"I haven't said anything against him," replied Baum, and Walpurga was obliged to admit that this was the case; nevertheless, she could not help feeling that any offer of love to another man's wife is an insult to her husband, for it implies as plainly as words can express it: "He is not the right man, for he has such and such faults; I alone am worthy of you."

Sighing deeply, Baum answered:

"Oh, if one could only double his life."

"I should think one life was enough for any man."

"Certainly, if one hasn't wasted it. One can only live once, you know."

"Yes, in this world; but in the next it begins anew."

"I mean in this world, too. But it's very hard, let me tell you, if one's whole life has been wasted through a stupid blunder. Must one bear with it and make no attempt to change it? We've both of us blundered."

"Who?"

"While I was a soldier, I became acquainted with the valet of the late king. He was very fond of me and took great pleasure in helping me forward; but he well knew what he was about. I thought it a wonderful piece of luck, when I found I was to marry his daughter. It was only too late, when I discovered that she was sickly and irritable and without a healthy drop of blood in her body. And is my whole life to be wasted, because of this blunder? And is no love left for me in the world? And with you, it's just the same; with both of us, you and I--but why should it be too late, even now?"

"Pretty jokes, indeed! but they're not to my taste. It's wrong to talk about such things."

"I'm not joking. Are all of earth's joys to be lost to us, just because we have once blundered? In that case, we'd be doubly fools."

"I see you're in earnest."

"Certainly I am," said Baum, his voice trembling with emotion.

"Very well, then. Just listen to what I've got to say. How can you dare insult my Hansei, that way? If it were so--and it isn't--but suppose it were; do you think, even if you were better looking or better mannered than my Hansei, and you're far from being that, let me tell you.--But that doesn't matter one way or the other. There's not a better man living than my Hansei, and even if there be one, he's nothing to me; we're husband and wife and belong to each other.--But it was only a joke, after all, wasn't it? and a mighty stupid one at that. Say that you only meant it for fun, for if I thought you were in earnest, I'd never speak another word to you; and now--Good-night."

"No, wait a moment. Now that I know how good you are, I think so much the more of you. If I only had a wife like you!"

Baum was greatly agitated. He had at first only dallied with kind words, but his voice had gradually assumed an agitated and touching tone.

"I'll give you something," said Walpurga, placing her hand on his shoulder.

"What is it; a kiss?"

"Get out! Don't talk so. You've just been behaving so well. Now I'll tell you something that my mother taught me. She always says, that he who is not contented with what he has, would be dissatisfied even if he had what he wished for."

"Did your mother tell you that?"

"Yes, and she knows many other good sayings, and I am glad that this one will be of use to you; it'll do you good."

"Of course--but now give me just one kiss, because I've been so good."

"What a foolish fellow you are," said Walpurga; "you say you're good, and, the very next minute, want something wicked as a reward. I'm a married woman and, if you were to give me a whole palace with all that's in it and seven palaces besides, I'd not kiss any man but my husband. There, I'll shake hands with you--and now--good-night."

They parted, with a mutual promise to remain good friends.

Walpurga found Mademoiselle Kramer in great trouble. The child was crying, and would not be pacified until Walpurga sang to it.

Meanwhile, Baum returned to the palace. He bit his lips with vexation and thought to himself: What a simple, stupid creature such a peasant woman is. And she is beautiful; I can wait; I know the long road; she shall be tamed yet.

For many days, Walpurga would pass Baum without looking up, and he, too, seemed shy; but one day, when she was sitting on the bench, he quickly said while passing:

"You needn't be angry at me; I didn't know I'd offended you and, if I have, I ask your pardon."

Walpurga looked up as if relieved. Baum nodded to her and hurried away.

CHAPTER XVI

The king had returned from the baths. He was received with great ceremony, but he and the queen soon withdrew from the company and repaired to the crown prince's apartments. The parents, clasping hands, stood by the cradle of the sleeping child. Their glances rested upon each other and then upon the prince.

"Can there be a higher joy than thus to behold the babe whose life belongs to and is a part of our own?" softly whispered the queen.

The king embraced her.

The child awoke; his cheeks were glowing, his eyes were bright.

In the mean while, Walpurga had been sitting in a corner, weeping silently; but now she was obliged to go to the child. The king left; the queen remained with her.

"You've been crying?" asked the queen.

"It was for joy, nothing but joy. Could anything be more beautiful than the way you stood together there?"

"I'll have your husband come to you," replied the queen; "write him to come, and say that your mother and child may come too."

"Yes, dear queen, it would be very nice, but it would cost a pretty penny." Surprised that any one was obliged to deny himself a pleasure, because of the expense, the queen looked up and said:

"Go to the paymaster and get the money. Would a hundred florins be enough?"

"Oh! More than enough! But if the queen would give me the money, we could make better use of it."

The queen looked at Walpurga, as if shocked to think that, even in simple hearts, avarice can destroy the noblest emotions.

Walpurga observed the change in the queen's expression and said:

"I'll tell you, honestly, why I don't want it, even if it cost nothing. My husband's a good man, but he's just a little bit awkward, and it would grieve him to the heart if any one were to laugh at him. And it would be too much to expect of mother, for she's over sixty years old, and hasn't been out of the village since her wedding-day--that is, not farther than Hohenheiligen, three miles from our place, where she went on a pilgrimage. Though it would only be a day's journey, she hasn't even once gone home in all that time; and so I think it might do her harm if she were taken anywhere else, even it were only for a few days. The best thing would be if we could all of us remain near the king. I'm sure we'd take good care of the dairy-farm. My husband knows all about cattle; he was cowboy for many years, and, afterward, herdsman on the mountain meadows."

Walpurga spoke as if the queen knew all about the plan, but the queen was so possessed with the thought of her domestic happiness, that she did not hear a word of what was said.

Days passed by, and Walpurga, who had received none of the traveling money that the queen had promised her, did not venture to ask the court paymaster for it. Desirous of showing Baum that she was still on friendly terms with him, she told him what had happened.

"The best thing you can do," said he, with a shrewd air, "is not to take so small a gift. If you do, they'll think they've done with you; don't lose sight of the main chance, and that's the farm."

Walpurga was sincerely grateful to Baum. It was very fortunate, she thought, to have a friend at the palace, who, while the king was yet a prince, had traveled with him through Italy and France, and who knew how one ought to deal with such high folk.

The palace seemed to have thrown off its tranquil ways of the last few weeks. All was life and bustle. Sounds of laughter and of song could be heard from early morn until late at night. Gay colored lamps hung from the trees and, at night, the sparkling lights seemed, in the distance, as if part of a fairy-scene.

Early in the morning, wagons laden with provisions could be seen going hither and thither. To-day, the court would dine on some wooded height; to-morrow, in a ravine, or near a waterfall.

The king was all kindness and attention to his wife, and the queen had never seemed more lovely in his eyes, than now, elevated as she was by maternal happiness and conjugal affection.

In the apartments occupied by Walpurga and Mademoiselle Kramer, none of this bustle of preparation or departure was heard. They simply knew that "all had gone off, for the day."

In the morning, while the day was still young, and in the evening, while the soft dews were falling, the king and queen, arm in arm, might often have been seen sauntering in the park, and at such times the ladies and gentlemen would remain near the palace.

One evening, while the king and queen were thus walking together, engaged in familiar conversation, the queen said:

"How delightful it is to be thus leaning on your arm; to close one's eyes and be led by you. You can't imagine what good it does me."

Although the king expressed himself delighted with her devotion, an inner voice told him that such sensibility was unqueenly. How differently--

No, he would not permit himself to think of it.

The queen had much to tell him of the gradual dawning of sense in the prince. He listened attentively, but rather through politeness than sympathy. After the first week, the queen excused herself from taking part in the frequent excursions, for she found no pleasure in all the bustle.

The queen had Walpurga and the child with her, either in the park or on the rising ground behind the palace, where she would sketch groups of trees, the lake and the swans, the castle, the chapel, and various distant views.

One morning, while at breakfast, the king said:

"What charming rivalry it was when you and Countess Irma were drawing together. Your dispositions were both illustrated by the way in which you treated the same subjects."

"Yes, we often remarked that. Perhaps I worked in the details more correctly and sharply, while Countess Irma sketched with far greater ease and freedom. I greatly miss the dear countess."

"Then let us write to her and tell her that she must return, and that at once. Let us send her a joint letter. Ladies and gentleman, we shall now, all of us, write a letter to Countess Irma."

"Order the writing materials to be brought," said he to one of the gentlemen in waiting. His request was speedily complied with and he wrote:

"Beautiful Countess! Fugitive bird! At last I know what bird you are:-- The wild dove. Does this contradiction describe you? Wild, and yet a dove? Come, do come to us; your forest companions hang their heads because of your absence. Hasten to us, on wings of song."

The king offered the sheet to the queen and said: "What will you write?"

"I can't write when any one is present," replied the queen. "I can't write a word now; I shall send her a separate letter."

An almost imperceptible expression of displeasure passed over the king's countenance, but he subdued it.

"As you please," said he courteously, although, at heart, angry at this everlasting sentimentalism.

The courtiers and ladies all wrote, each adding a few lines of a light, jesting character.

Countess Brinkenstein, however, had slipped away.

Amid jests and laughter, the whole sheet was at last filled, and then the king said:

"The chief one is still missing. Walpurga must also write to the countess, for the voice of the people has most influence with her. Send Walpurga here."

Baum was at once sent to bring Walpurga. On the way, he explained to her what was going on. Walpurga was not shy, in the midst of the assembled court.

"Would you rather be alone in your room while you write?" asked the king, betraying his vexation, in spite of himself.

"I'll write wherever you want me to, but I can't do it well."

Walpurga seated herself and wrote:

"If your noble father will allow it, I shall be heartily glad when my dear Countess Irma is here again. My heart longs for her.

"Walpurga Andermatten."

The king, having read it, said: "Write also--'it will do me and the prince much good to have you here again. You make us both happier'."

"Dear king," said Walpurga, "how clever you are. What you say is quite true. Now be so kind as to dictate it to me. I can't put it into such good words, but I can write quite well from dictation. I learned it from Mademoiselle Kramer. I used to know how at school, but forgot it afterward."

"No," replied the king, "write as your feelings prompt you. Ladies and gentlemen, let us leave Walpurga alone, and go to the veranda."

Walpurga was sitting alone, in the great breakfast-room, biting the end of her pen and vainly endeavoring to remember the king's words. Suddenly she heard a slight noise near her and, looking up, saw Baum who was standing in the doorway.

"Come here," she exclaimed, "you can help me, for you must have heard it all."

"Certainly," replied Baum and dictated the king's words to Walpurga. She went out and handed the letter to the king.

He praised her for having put the words so nicely. She was about to say that Baum had helped her, but one need not tell everything, and why not receive praise for what might have been?

When Walpurga returned to her room, she smiled at her own shrewdness. The king would now surely give her the farm, for he had seen that she could write down everything and could keep accounts.

The queen came into the garden with her hastily written note.

It was unsealed. She gave it to the king saying:

"Will you read it?"

"It isn't necessary," said the king, closing the letter.

After the letter was written there was endless tittering among the court ladies. They chirruped and chattered and teased each other, and hopped about like a flock of sparrows that have just discovered an open sack of corn. They soon scattered, and ladies who at other times could not endure each other were now good friends and, arm in arm, would walk up and down the park, while others would stand gathered in little groups. All seemed loth to separate. They had so much to tell each other that none seemed willing to leave. They all spoke kindly of Irma. Every one was still her best friend, but, nevertheless, careful to leave a loophole of escape open, for things might change.

Within a few days, a great change had come over the feelings of all at the summer palace. The king and queen had, at first, greeted each other as if newly married, as if unspeakably happy; but, soon afterward, came the first distinct sense of uncongeniality which, in a word, betokened that the king wearied of the queen. He did full justice to her noble and exalted appearance. Her every word and thought was an outgush of purest emotion. But this exaltation of feeling, which, to an every-day world, appears strange and incomprehensible and yet exacts constant consideration for its peculiarities; this endeavor to give intense and exhaustive thought to every casual subject; this utter absence of all cheerful or sportive traits; this cathedral-like solemnity of character; this constant dwelling on the heights: though beautiful and engaging at times, had become monotonous and distasteful to the king. The queen's conversation lacked that sparkling effervescence which, though it be only for a moment, charms and animates the listener.

The king who was fond of change, delighted in what was sportive, capricious, or enigmatical in character, and in the conquering of difficulties.

The remembrance of Irma supplied all that he missed in the queen. He felt sure of his faithful love for his wife, but admired the frank and lovely disposition of Irma, and why should he not, therefore, enjoy her society?

"She will come and remain with us, and bring new and fresh life with her," thought he to himself when he saw the courier who bore the letter to Irma, hurrying along the road.

In the afternoon, the king and queen drove out together; he sat at her side and held the reins. Their only attendants were the two grooms who followed on horseback.

The king was quite amiable; the queen happy. He felt inwardly conscious of having, in ever so slight a degree, swerved from the right path, and this made him doubly affectionate. With a frank gaze, he looked into the brightly beaming eyes of his beautiful wife.

Thus should it ever be. Thus, purely and frankly, shouldst thou ever be able to look into those eyes.

CHAPTER XVII

"Your Majesty," said Countess Brinkenstein, on the following morning when they were sauntering in the park, "I owe you an explanation for not having signed the letter to the queen's maid of honor."

"You did not?" replied the king.

The rigid yet refined features of the old lady showed no change at these words, although she might have felt wounded at the intimation that the absence of her signature had not been remarked. But, in all things, she obeyed the highest law of the courtier; that is, to repress all personal feeling and thus avoid all sensitiveness. Couching her censure in terms of praise, in according with courtly fashion, she calmly added:

"The idea of the invitation was quite original, but genius must ever stand alone. Your Majesty has often honored me by addressing me as your motherly friend and, as such, you will, I trust, permit me to remark that it does not become either the gentlemen or the ladies to put their names to an extraordinary jest of Your Majesty's. There should not be the slightest cause for suspicion that this invitation was designedly open and informal, because secretly intended and wished for."

The king looked at the old lady in surprise, but acted as if unconscious of her having seen through his disguise.

"I must again tell you, my lady, that you ought to have gone to the baths. You take such somber and serious views of everything; but when one has been at the baths, as I have, everything looks gay and happy."

"Your Majesty, it is simply my duty to emphasize the rules that govern Your Majesty's high position."

"Are you not overdoing it?"

"Your Majesty, etiquette, although invisible, is none the less valuable. Treasures of artistic and great historical value are not melted over to make new coins, but are carefully handed down from century to century. The palace is the highest point in the land, where one is in full view of all, and where we should so live that we can afford to have all our actions seen."

The king was listless, for his mind wandered to Irma, who must now be receiving the letter. "She has awakened," thought he, "and is standing alone, or sitting beside her misanthropic father, on the balcony of the mountain castle. The letter comes, and she feels as if surrounded by a flock of chirruping, singing birds, that alight on her hands, her shoulders and her head. What a pity that one cannot behold her charming smile!"

The king's vision had been a true one. Irma was sitting beside her father and dreamily gazing into the distance. What was to become of her? If her father, would only say: "You must stay here." But this being obliged to decide for herself was the trouble. If she had a husband to command her--but Baron Schoning would have been her subject, and that would have made life's load a doubled one. At that moment, the housekeeper announced a messenger who had just arrived on horseback.

The courier entered, delivered his letter and said that he would await an answer. Irma read it and laughed aloud. She laid the letter on her lap, took it up again, and read and laughed again. Her father looked at her in surprise.

"What's the matter?"

"Read this."

The father read it; his expression did not change in the least.

"What do you mean to do?" he asked.

"I think I must obey such requests; but can I return without incurring your reproof?"

"Always; if there be nothing in your own heart to reprove you."

Irma rang for the housekeeper and told her to order the maid to make the necessary preparations for her departure; she also ordered them to treat the courier with hospitality, and to inform him that a part of the journey was to be accomplished the same evening. "Are you angry at me, father?"

"I am never angry. I am only sorry that so few persons allow their reason to guide them. But be calm, my child. If your resolve is dictated by reason you must follow it and bear the consequences calmly, just as I do. But let us spend the few hours yet left us, in peace and quiet; life lies in the present."

Irma gave many instructions to her maid and the courier, although it always seemed to her as if she were forgetting something which would not occur to her until after she had left.

Father and daughter were still at dinner. The carriage, laden with the luggage, had been sent forward a short distance to await them in the valley. The father accompanied Irma down the mountain. He spoke with her in a cheerful strain. While passing the apple-tree, on the way, he said:

"My child, let us take leave of each other here. This is the tree that I planted on the day you were born. It often marks the limit of my evening walk."

They stood there in silence. An apple fell from the tree and struck the ground at their feet. The father picked it up and gave it to his daughter.

"Take this fruit of your native soil with you. The apple falls from the tree because it is ripe, and because the tree has nothing more to give it. In the same way, man leaves home and kindred; but a human being is more than the fruit of the tree. And now, my child, take off your hat, and let me once more place my hands upon your head. No one knows when his hour will come. Nay, my child, do not weep. Nay, weep; and may you, through life, only have to weep for others, but never for yourself." His voice faltered, but, recovering himself, he continued:

"And just as I now rest my hands upon your head and would fain place them on all your thoughts, do you ever remain true unto yourself. I would like to give you all my thoughts, but, for the present, keep this one in your memory: Indulge in no pleasures but those which you can remember with pleasure. Take this kiss--you kiss passionately--may you never give a kiss in which your soul is less pure than at this moment. Farewell!"

The father turned away and walked up the mountain road. He did not look back again.

Irma looked after him, trembling and feeling as if something drew her toward home and bade her remain there forever. But she felt ashamed of her indecision; she thought of the next hour and of how strange it would seem to the servants and to her father, to see her trunks unpacked and all the preparation for the journey undone. No, it was too late, and she went on. She seated herself in the carriage and was soon on her journey. She was no longer her own mistress; a strange power had taken possession of her.

It was on the following day, at noon, that Irma reached the summer palace. All was quiet; no one came to meet her but the old steward, who hurriedly laid aside his long pipe.

"Where are their highnesses?" asked the courier.

"They dine at the Devil's Pulpit to-day."

From the garden, there resounded a cry.

"Oh, my countess! My countess is here!" exclaimed Walpurga, kissing Irma's hands and weeping for joy. "Now we'll have sunshine! Now we'll have day!"

Irma quieted the excited woman, who said:

"I'll go and tell the queen at once. She's the only one at home, and is up on yonder hill, painting; she doesn't care to go on these holiday excursions, and here every day seems a holiday."

Irma instructed Walpurga not to tell the queen, and said that she would join her. She went to her room and sat there for a long while, buried in thought. She felt as if she had extended a friendly hand and that no one had clasped it in return.

In the hallway, they were moving trunks about. Suddenly, she thought of the time when she sat in her room, an orphan child, clad in black, and heard them moving her mother's coffin about in the adjoining apartment.

Why had it occurred to her at that moment? She arose--she could no longer endure being alone. She hastily changed her dress and went to the queen.

The queen saw her coming and advanced to meet her.

Irma bent low and made an effort to kiss her hand.

The queen held her up and, embracing her, imprinted a tender kiss upon her lips.

"You're the only one who dare touch the lips that my father has kissed," said Irma--that is, she did not say it aloud, but simply moved her lips as if forming the words. Deep within her soul, arose a thought: I'd rather die a thousand deaths, than sadden that guileless heart.

The thought illumined her countenance with a noble expression, and the queen, all delight, exclaimed:

"Oh how beautiful, how radiant you are, Countess Irma!"

Irma dropped her eyes and knelt down beside the child's cradle. Her eyes were so lustrous that the child put out its hand as if to seize them.

"He's right," said Walpurga, "he tries to catch the light already, but I think your eyes have grown larger than they used to be."

Irma went with Walpurga and excused herself for not having visited the cottage by the lake. She then told her of her friend in the convent.

"And how's your father?" asked Walpurga.

Irma was startled. The queen had not even inquired about her father. Walpurga was the only one who had asked about him.

She told her that he knew her mother, and also her uncle, who often burnt pitch in the forest.

"Yes, he's my mother's brother; so you know him, too?"

"I don't, but my father does."

Walpurga told her about her uncle Peter, who was known as the "little pitchman," and vowed that she would send him something, one of these days, for the poor old fellow had a hard time of it in this world. Old Zenza had had the courage to come to the palace, but the little pitchman would starve to death before he would do such a thing.

While Walpurga was speaking, the queen went to the cradle, and when the prince saw her, he struggled, with hands and feet, as if trying to get to her. She bent down and raised him up, and Walpurga exclaimed:

"Dear me! on the very day our countess returns, our prince sits up for the first time. Yes, she can make everything go right."

The queen and Irma remained together in cheerful and unconstrained conversation. In the evening, there were joyful greetings on the part of those who had returned from the excursion to the Devil's Pulpit. Irma now, for the first time, learned that her brother was not at court. While at the baths, he had made the acquaintance of Baroness Steigeneck and her daughter and was now visiting them.

The king's greeting of Irma was quite formal. Even Countess Brinkenstein could have found nothing to object to in it; but how could he well have done otherwise, when the queen said:

"I can't tell you how happy our dear countess's return has made me; we've already spent several delightful hours together."

In the evening, there were fireworks which the king had ordered to be prepared in honor of Irma's arrival. Far and near, the people were looking at the lights and the gay-colored sheets of fire ascending heavenward. At last, Countess Irma's name stood forth in letters of fire, held aloft by mountaineers. The flame crackled, and, from behind the shrubbery, there issued strains of music which were echoed back from the distance. In the midst of all this noise and splendor, Irma was ever asking herself: "How fares it now with your father?"

Count Eberhard, in his mountain castle, was sitting by the window and, looking out into the starry night, said to himself: "Just as the stars above are separate and distinct from each other, so is every human soul solitary and alone. Each travels in its own orbit, its course determined by the attraction and repulsion of the heavenly bodies that environ it."

That night, Irma dreamt that a star descended from heaven and fell upon her bosom. She tried to grasp it, but it eluded her and transformed itself into a human figure which, with averted glance, exclaimed: "Thou, too, art solitary."